Gabe Deveraux on baby-making with Maggie Calloway…

Sperm donor?

She's lost her mind if she thinks I would just stand by and let her use the services of an anonymous sperm donor! A beautiful gal like Maggie deserves to know her baby's father. Maggie should be loved and cherished by a good man worthy of her love, one who has won her heart.

Maggie is as stubborn as she is lovely. So it's going to take a bit of strategizing to convince her to change her mind. I am more than willing to be her baby's father. Only, there's no way that the birth of any child of mine would be the direct result of my utilizing something as sterile and impersonal as a sperm bank!

We're going to have to do this the old-fashioned way.

Dear Reader,

Millionaire. Prince. Secret agent. Doctor. If any—or all—of these men strike your fancy, well…you're in luck! These fabulous guys are waiting for you in the pages of this month's offerings from Harlequin American Romance.

His best friend's request to father her child leads millionaire Gabe Deveraux to offer a bold marriage proposal in *My Secret Wife* by Cathy Gillen Thacker, the latest installment of THE DEVERAUX LEGACY series. A royal request makes Prince Jace Carradigne heir to a throne—and in search of his missing fiancée—in Mindy Neff's *The Inconveniently Engaged Prince*, part of our ongoing series THE CARRADIGNES: AMERICAN ROYALTY. (And there are royals galore to be found when the series comes to a sensational ending in *Heir to the Throne*, a special two-in-one collection by Kasey Michaels and Carolyn Davidson, available next month wherever Harlequin books are sold.)

Kids, kangaroos and a kindhearted woman are all in a day's work for cool and collected secret agent Mike Wheeler in *Secret Service Dad*, the second book in Mollie Molay's GROOMS IN UNIFORM series. And a big-city doctor attempts to hide his true identity—and his affections—for a Montana beauty in *The Doctor Wore Boots* by Debra Webb, the conclusion to the TRADING PLACES duo.

So be sure to catch all of these wonderful men this month—and every month—as you enjoy their wonderful love stories from Harlequin American Romance.

Happy reading,

Melissa Jeglinski
Associate Senior Editor
Harlequin American Romance

Cathy Gillen Thacker

MY SECRET WIFE

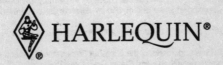

TORONTO • NEW YORK • LONDON
AMSTERDAM • PARIS • SYDNEY • HAMBURG
STOCKHOLM • ATHENS • TOKYO • MILAN • MADRID
PRAGUE • WARSAW • BUDAPEST • AUCKLAND

This book is for my mom and dad,
who, in the last year, have shown me
what courage, determination and the power of love
are all about.

ISBN 0-373-16945-0

MY SECRET WIFE

Copyright © 2002 by Cathy Gillen Thacker.

Visit us at www.eHarlequin.com

Printed in U.S.A.

ABOUT THE AUTHOR

Cathy Gillen Thacker married her high school sweetheart and hasn't had a dull moment since. Why, you ask? Well, there were three kids, various pets, any number of automobiles, several moves across the country, his and her careers, and sundry other experiences. But mostly, there was love and friendship and laughter, and lots of experiences she wouldn't trade for the world.

You can find out more about Cathy and her books at www.cathygillenthacker.com, and you can write her c/o Harlequin Books, 300 East 42nd Street, New York, NY 10017.

Books by Cathy Gillen Thacker

HARLEQUIN AMERICAN ROMANCE

HARLEQUIN BOOKS

Who's Who
in the Deveraux Family

Tom Deveraux—The head of the family and CEO of the Deveraux shipping empire that has been handed down through the generations.

Grace Deveraux—Estranged from Tom for years, but back in town—after a personal tragedy—for some much-needed family support.

Chase Deveraux—The eldest son and the biggest playboy in the greater Charleston area.

Mitch Deveraux—A chip off the old block and about to double the size of the family business via a business/marriage arrangement.

Dr. Gabe Deveraux—The "Goodest" Samaritan around. Any damsels in distress in need of the good doctor's assistance…?

Amy Deveraux—The baby sister. She's determined to reunite her parents.

Winnifred Deveraux Smith—Tom's widowed sister. The social doyenne of Charleston, she's determined never to marry. That's not what she has in mind for her niece and nephews, though.

Herry Bowles—The butler. Distinguished, indispensable and devoted to his boss, Winnifred.

Eleanor—The Deveraux ancestor with whom the legacy of ill-fated love began.

Chapter One

Gabe Deveraux met Maggie Callaway halfway down the steps to his beach house and regarded her with embarrassment. "Thanks for coming," he said, waving as the last of the Isle of Palms fire trucks drove away.

"You said it was an emergency." Maggie looked at the charred interior of the rear of his house, then turned back to him. She was dressed as she always was when working—in work boots, nice-fitting jeans, a long-sleeved cotton shirt and an open khaki vest with multiple pockets. Her honey-blond hair framed her piquant face in tousled waves. Her kissable lips were softly glossed, her lively light-green eyes alight with interest as she looked him over from head to toe. "What happened here?" she asked, her gaze roving the wrinkled state of his clothes before returning once again to his unshaven jaw and weary eyes. At five foot five, she was some seven inches shorter than he was. "Did you finally decide to learn how to cook?"

Gabe grimaced and shoved a hand through the short layers of his hair as he led Maggie all the way inside. "Actually, I'm not really sure how it happened," he admitted.

"Well, I am." Penny Stringfield emerged from the master bedroom on the second floor and walked down the hallway overlooking the first floor to the stairs. The petite redhead was dressed in a hospital nurse's uniform and carried a suitcase in one hand, a smaller toiletries bag in the other. "I put some soup on to boil and then forgot about it," Penny explained to both Maggie and Gabe as she came down the staircase and walked over to them. "The pan boiled dry and the wallpaper caught fire, and the next thing I knew it was time to dial 911."

Her face filled with regret, Penny set her things down, propelled herself into Gabe's arms and hugged him fiercely. Over the top of her head, Gabe saw Maggie's faintly disapproving expression as she watched what was going on between him and his houseguest.

"I'm so sorry, Gabe," Penny said, in a voice still scratchy from the voluminous tears she had shed the night before. "I never meant to set your kitchen on fire while you were at the hospital. Especially after last night. If you hadn't been here for me, well, I don't know what I would have done."

"I was glad to help," Gabe said, knowing even as he spoke the soothing words how they would likely be misinterpreted by Maggie. He grasped Penny's shoulders and drew her back so she had no choice but to look into his face. "You know that. But—"

"But nothing," Penny sniffed indignantly. "I'm moving to a hotel now."

"You don't have to do that," he said firmly. Recalling how devastated Penny had been the night before, when she had first showed up on his doorstep, Gabe's heart went out to her. Although why Penny felt that Lane Stringfield was about to stop loving her, Gabe still didn't know, because she hadn't explained. All he knew for sure was that Penny was very upset, very frightened and agitated, and still very in love with Lane. People in that condition needed a friend. And since he was the one Penny had turned to, he felt bound to do whatever was necessary to help her.

"Yes, I do, Gabe." Fleeting regret crossed Penny's face, as she wiped her tears away. "We both know it's for the best," she said, pausing to blow her nose delicately. "I never should have agreed to stay here with you in the first place. The last thing I want to do is drag you into the middle of the breakup of my marriage."

Gabe wasn't so sure the Stringfield union was ending—after all, the two had been man and wife for five years now. Happily espoused, as far as he and everyone else could see. Surely, whatever the misunderstanding was, it could be cleared up.

Catching the curious, slightly jealous expression on

Maggie's face out of the corner of his eye, Gabe faced his houseguest determinedly and tried again. "Penny—"

"I'll be fine, Gabe." Penny stepped back and away from Gabe. "Really. I'm not so sure about your kitchen, however."

"Oh, we can fix that," Maggie said, already eyeing the devastation with a professional kitchen designer's unerring eye.

"Good. Because I want to help pay for it," Penny said emphatically. She picked up her bags, stepped past. "I'll talk to you later, at the hospital, Gabe."

Gabe waited until Penny had driven away, then turned back to Maggie. As he had suspected, she did not look happy with him at all. "It's not what you think," he said quietly, guessing from the downturned corners of her soft lips what her thoughts were. "Penny Stringfield and I are not romantically involved." He had not come between Lane and Penny the way he had inadvertently come between Maggie and his brother, when she and Chase were just days from saying "I Do."

Maggie shrugged her slender shoulders as she plucked a small spiral notepad from one of the pockets of her khaki cargo vest. "Did I say you caused the breakup of Penny's marriage?" she said coolly as she removed a pen from another pocket, flipped back the cover on her notepad and began to scribble notes to herself.

"You didn't have to." Gabe followed Maggie around as she inspected the damage the licking flames had done to his appliances, cabinets, walls and windows. Although all were still standing, all were so smoke-, flame- and water-damaged they were going to have to be ripped out and replaced. Needing some fresh air, Gabe tried to open the window and found the frame so warped it wouldn't open. He went to the patio door opposite and opened that to let more fresh ocean air blow in. "I can tell by the look on your face that you've jumped to the conclusion that I'm responsible," he continued as the first floor filled with the cool ocean breeze. "But it's not true. Penny and I are just friends. All I was trying to do was help her out by giving her a place to crash until she calmed down." And came to her senses, Gabe added mentally.

"Look, Gabe, it's really none of my business." Careful not to back up against anything, Maggie tipped her head back and studied the soot clinging to every inch of his kitchen ceiling, "Since you and I are just friends, too."

"Yeah, well, that wasn't really my choice now, was it?" Gabe said, as Maggie squatted down and tested the vinyl tile that had melted into the water-logged floorboard beneath it. "I wanted to date you." And, in fact, had asked her out several times during the past few weeks, only to be turned down with one flimsy excuse after another.

Exasperation swept into Maggie's high, delicately boned cheeks as she stood. Propping one hand on her hip, she squared off with him again. "We have to face it, Gabe, whether we want to or not." Regret shimmered in her pretty long-lashed eyes. "I caused your entire family a great deal of unhappiness when I broke off my plans to marry your brother just days before we were to walk down the aisle, and I did it because I was attracted to you."

Fresh guilt flooded Gabe. He refused to let it get to him as he met Maggie's gaze, bluntly and emphatically reminding her of the reconciliation that had taken place a few weeks prior, after two years of considerable familial unrest. "Chase has forgiven us."

"But I'm not so sure the rest of your family has, or ever will," Maggie replied. "Nor can I say I blame them. The whole episode was really humiliating and embarrassing for everyone. And we only made it worse when we tried to date, immediately after I ended it with your older brother. So I think, for a lot of reasons, it's best we continue just to be friends."

Gabe sighed.

Intellectually, he knew Maggie was right. His parents, sister Amy and brother Mitch were a long way from ever forgiving Maggie for the acrimony she had caused his already broken family. It didn't stop him from wanting her. Nor her, he guessed, from wanting him. That had been proven weeks ago, when, without warning, they had met to talk about something else and suddenly found themselves kissing again. And worse, been spotted by Chase when they were doing so!

Emotionally, he still wanted her—for reasons he had yet to closely examine. Reasons he probably didn't want to examine.

"So back to why you called me here," Maggie said, commandeering Gabe's attention once again. "What is it exactly that you want me to do for you?" she asked in a crisp, all-business tone that let Gabe know in an instant that any fantasies he might still be harboring about the two of them were not about to come true, now or at any other time.

Gabe grimaced and pushed his disappointment aside, looked her straight in the eye and directed just as firmly, "I want all the damage cleared away, and my kitchen put back the way it was as soon as possible. So. Now that you know what I want—" Gabe regarded Maggie impatiently, folding his arms in front of him "—how fast can you do it?"

WASN'T THAT JUST LIKE rich boy Gabe Deveraux, Maggie thought. To want *what* he wanted *when* he wanted it. Damn the consequences. "Right now, I've got a four-month waiting list," she said, a trifle impatiently.

Gabe shoved a hand through his midnight-black

hair. His distress showed in his boyishly handsome face. "I can't live like this. I need my house repaired right away." He fastened his gaze on her face. "Isn't there anything you can do to speed things up?"

Maggie had to turn away from the seductive expression in his blue-gray eyes. "Sure." She shrugged, telling herself she was immune to the desire that shimmered through her whenever she was this close to his lean and athletic six-foot frame, now that she had learned the hard way that his interest in her would always be only a fleeting—and hence hurtful—thing. "But it would cost you double time."

Gabe beamed. "Done!" he said enthusiastically.

Maggie told herself she was only accommodating Gabe's wishes to help boost the profits of the home-remodeling-business-turned-kitchen-design emporium she had inherited from her mother and father the year before. She didn't want to spend time with him, or do anything that would further the mounting sexual tension between them. Which was why she had avoided seeing Gabe—and everyone else in his family—until about a month ago, when a medical problem had prompted her to call Gabe, to get some advice—and a referral—she could trust.

He had come through for her that afternoon, as she had known he would.

But he had also kissed her.

And stirred up a lot of feelings she hadn't wanted to feel.

Since then, Gabe and his brother Chase had made up and agreed to let the past be just that. Which left Gabe wanting to date her again. But knowing Gabe never dated any one woman for more than a few weeks, if that long, Maggie had declined. Repeatedly.

And she was glad she had.

She didn't want her heart broken by Gabe again.

Aware Gabe was waiting for her to continue, Maggie said, ''I can get the guys to start clearing out the charred rubble this morning. But we won't be able to do anything more than that until I clear it with the client whose job I was to begin tomorrow morning.''

''Just do what you can as fast as you can,'' Gabe said with a frown.

While Maggie was on the phone with the next client on her waiting list, Gabe's brother Chase arrived. As she watched her former fiancé, now a happily married man, mount the steps to Gabe's beach house, which was just a mile or so from Chase's own, Maggie thought how odd it was to have no feeling at all for Chase, except maybe a lingering warmth—the kind you had for a guy who had once been your boyfriend, but who now was merely a casual acquaintance. Had she ever really loved Chase Deveraux, surely she would have felt more for him now. But she didn't. Which only went to show, Maggie thought dispiritedly, that she really didn't know anything about what the love between a man and a woman should be after all.

"Hey, Mags," Chase said with a smile the moment Maggie got off her cell phone. "I've got a proposition for you. I want to do a story on this kitchen fire and a before-and-after photo-spread of the renovation for *Modern Man* magazine. Interested?"

"I wouldn't mind the free advertising," Maggie said. The magazine Chase published was one of the hottest publications for men. A lot of women read it, too.

Chase nodded, pleased. "Great. I'll send Daisy Templeton over on a daily basis to photograph the work in progress."

The pager attached to Gabe's belt went off. "It's the hospital. Excuse me for a minute."

Maggie and Chase stepped outside on the deck to give Gabe the privacy he needed while talking to the hospital. Chase looked at Maggie curiously. "So what's going on between the two of you?" he asked, abruptly becoming more protective older brother to Gabe, than ex-fiancé to Maggie. "Are you dating now or what?"

Maggie had the feeling a part of Chase would have been relieved if they had been—it would have been easier on his male ego had she and his younger brother not been able to keep their hands off each other. It would have explained once and for all why she'd left him at the altar to be with Gabe. Because everyone knew Maggie wasn't the type of woman to string any man along.

"Gabe and I are just friends, Chase," Maggie responded quietly. And not very good ones at that, Maggie thought, given the continuing sexual tension between them. The fact their relationship was unrequited and destined to stay that way made a strictly platonic relationship between her and Gabe all but impossible.

"That's too bad." Chase's disappointment was evident. Maggie knew Chase had hoped his forgiveness would spur her and Gabe on to a more meaningful relationship. "I want Gabe to be with his dream woman," Chase said seriously. "And I've thought for a while now that woman was you."

"Well, it's not," Maggie said briskly, recalling all too well how swiftly and remorselessly Gabe had dumped her. "But thanks for caring enough to want to see your brother happy," she said sincerely, relieved that Chase was no longer angry with her for the mistakes she had made when she was engaged to him.

Chase rested his hands on her shoulders. "I want to see you both happy, Mags. As happy as Bridgett and I are," Chase said firmly.

"I want that, too," Maggie said. She just didn't see how it would ever happen with her and Gabe, no matter what Chase and his new bride Bridgett hoped.

Chase then headed off for the magazine office, and Maggie got her laptop computer out of her truck. By the time she had walked back into the living room, which, thanks to the quick response of the fire department as well as the judicial use of a fire extinguisher on the blaze in the kitchen had remained unscathed, Gabe was just getting off the phone.

"Sorry about that. I had a patient admitted last night. We don't know who she is. She's eighty-something and obviously confused. I was hoping the police would have been able to connect her with a missing persons report, but so far, nothing."

"Is she going to be all right?"

"I hope so. But we have to figure out what's wrong with Jane Doe first, and that's not easy to do when we don't have a medical history on her, and she isn't able to explain to us how she ended up in the historic district with a sprained ankle in the middle of the night, or even how long she was lying there on the sidewalk before the newspaper delivery person happened along and found her. But she's such a lovely lady I can't imagine she could go missing for very long. So I'm sure it'll all be worked out in a matter of hours."

Maggie frowned as she mulled over the dilemma. "You could always get the TV stations involved," she suggested.

"We will, believe me, if we don't get some answers soon." Gabe turned his intent blue-gray gaze on her. "And speaking of medical situations—how are you?"

MAGGIE HAD BEEN HOPING Gabe wouldn't bring that up.

It was bad enough she had called him for advice and broken down in his arms; his pity for her had led to the infamous kiss on the beach that Chase had seen—and a lot of family turmoil between Gabe and his brother Chase. True, that conflict had since been resolved, but she was still embarrassed about the way she had bared her soul to Gabe that day. It wasn't like her to reveal her deepest hurts or darkest fears to anyone. She preferred giving off a self-possessed, independent aura. No way was she a vulnerable woman in need of a man to lean on. Steeling herself against the kindness in his eyes, Maggie swallowed, and said, "I saw the physician you recommended."

"And…?" Gabe tensed as he waited for her reply.

"I have severe endometriosis." Maggie turned her back to the three Callaway Kitchen Construction trucks pulling up in the drive. She folded her arms in front of her and faced Gabe with as much courage as she could muster. "If I want to bear a child, and I do, very much, it's recommended that I get pregnant as soon as possible."

Gabe looked first stunned—then accepting over the news of her impending parenthood. "Who's the lucky dad?" he asked casually, thrusting his hands in the pockets of his slacks, as truck doors opened and shut and heavy work boots clopped up the beach-house steps.

Maggie hedged, aware the next part was even more embarrassing. "I don't know yet," she said, biting her lower lip. "I have to visit the sperm bank this afternoon and pick one out."

Gabe stared at her as if she had suddenly grown two heads. "You're kidding, right?"

Maggie pretended a great deal more insouciance than she felt. "It's either that or the old-fashioned way," she said with a confident tilt of her head. "And since time is of the essence and I'm not currently even dating anyone…" She shrugged her slender shoulders and let her words trail off.

She could tell by the disapproving look on his face that Gabe was about to tell her what a mistake she was making. Fortunately, he had no chance to do so as they were joined by Maggie's electrician, Enrico Chavez, his brother, master plumber Manuel Chavez, and her carpenter and cabinetmaker Luis Chavez. The three brothers were all in their fifties. They had worked for Maggie's dad and mom for years, and now they worked for Maggie. Devout Catholics, family men, they were fiercely protective of her. They were also, after the sudden deaths of her parents the previous year, the only "family" Maggie had, and she treasured the way they looked out for her, just as she did her best to look out for the three Chavez brothers and their families.

"Hi, guys," Maggie said, as she physically aligned herself with Gabe to better make introductions and talk to her crew. "This is Gabe Deveraux. He's a critical care doc over at Charleston Hospital, and it's his kitchen we're going to be working on here." Glad to have something else to talk about, Maggie finished the introductions and then explained briefly what was going to need to be done, once the new design was settled on, and when.

"What about the Hegameyer job?" Luis asked, concerned.

Realizing she was standing almost too close to Gabe, Maggie moved slightly away from his tall, strong frame. "The Hegameyers have generously agreed to wait another four months."

"How'd you get them to agree to that?" Manuel asked, dark brow furrowing.

"I promised to cut fifty percent off their labor costs. Not to worry though," Maggie added hastily, reading the worry on Enrico's face, "Gabe here is going to pay us double time for labor for the entire project so we'll still come out at least fifty percent ahead. I plan to split the additional profit four ways, so we'll all come out better off." Her parents had taught her the first rule of running a successful small business was to treat your employees as well as you treated yourself. She wanted them all to benefit.

"Sounds good to me," Enrico said. Luis and Manuel nodded, too.

"Well, I need to get going," Maggie said. Before

Gabe could delay her further, she rushed down the steps to her own pickup truck.

"THIS IS ALL your fault, you know," Manuel Chavez said the moment Maggie had driven off.

"What do you mean?" Gabe turned to the three men in surprise. Now that Maggie was gone, her employees seemed ready to string him up by his thumbs.

"If not for you," Luis said practically, "Maggie would have been married to your brother two years ago, and probably would have already had a baby when her parents died last year. But because of your selfish actions, Maggie's wedding to Chase did not happen. And now she's in an emotional tailspin, without any family at all, and going against nature to have a child."

"She told you about that?"

The Chavez brothers nodded. "We're family to her."

As much as Gabe was loathe to admit it, the three Chavez brothers had a right to be concerned. Two years ago, Maggie never would have considered what she was considering now, even if she had been facing infertility. Two years ago, she had known babies should be conceived in love, by two people who cared about each other, not by strangers in a science lab. "What do you want me to do?" Gabe asked gruffly, doubting Maggie would listen to him even if he did try to talk her out of getting pregnant this way.

Manuel's dark eyes glittered in abject disapproval. "We want you to do whatever you have to do to make it right."

"And keep Maggie from making a mistake she will regret the rest of her life," Luis added, scowling.

Enrico crossed his burly arms in front of his chest. "We're going to be watching you. Because no way are we letting you hurt our Maggie again."

That was just it, Gabe thought miserably. He didn't want to hurt Maggie. Never had. But he—a guy who prided himself on helping people—had done so just the same. The question was, how could he make it right and get Maggie to come to her senses? The men who worked for her were correct—Gabe owed her that and more, for the havoc he'd created in her life.

Chapter Two

"What are you doing here?" Maggie asked in surprise as Gabe walked up to her in the crowded fertility clinic waiting room.

She made room for him and he sat down beside her, his expression as tense and serious as her own. "I thought you might want some help screening prospective donors," he said.

Maggie wasn't thrilled to be picking out a father for her baby at a sperm bank, but if she wanted to have a baby of her own, and she did, it was something that had to be done, before she lost her ability to have a child forever. She turned slightly so she could see the expression on Gabe's face. Seating was tight, and her knee nudged his in the process. "Does that mean you approve of what I'm doing?" She studied him warily.

Gabe shrugged his broad shoulders casually. "It's not up to me to approve or disapprove," he said quietly. "It's your decision. I'm just here to support you in any way I can."

His words certainly seemed sincere enough, Maggie thought. Nevertheless, her gut feeling told her that Gabe wasn't any happier about her plan than anyone else who knew about it. Everyone thought she should wait. Give love and the prospect of marriage another try. Unfortunately, Maggie sighed to herself, it wasn't that easy finding a man she was attracted to physically, emotionally and intellectually. In fact, to date, there had only been one man who had caught her attention in all three ways, and that had been Gabe.

Not that it mattered, since Gabe's attention span when it came to women was notoriously short. According to those who knew him, Gabe hadn't dated any women for longer than a few weeks, if that, since high school. These days, he got involved with women—like Penny Stringfield—who needed help. Which he selflessly gave. When they were okay again, he moved on to the next damsel in distress.

Maggie had been one of those damsels in distress once, just prior to her wedding to Chase. She'd been having a lot of doubts leading up to the wedding that wasn't. But only Gabe had seen those qualms for what they really were—the gut-wrenching realization that she couldn't marry Chase because she didn't really love Chase any more than Chase really loved her.

She just hadn't known how to tell everyone that, including—and especially—Chase.

Had Gabe not seen her conundrum and stepped in to her rescue, encouraging her to speak what was in her heart and mind and then act on it, well…Maggie might well have married—and eventually been divorced from—his brother. Or at least she might have made it all the way down the aisle before coming to her senses and bolting.

But Gabe had come to her rescue.

And stood by her during all the social and family hubbub afterward, even going so far as to date her— twice—before deciding that that wasn't such a good idea after all.

Maggie had been deeply disappointed—for by then she had developed quite a crush on Gabe—but she had known, intellectually anyway, that Gabe was right. His brother Chase had been humiliated enough by Maggie's actions, without Gabe and Maggie making the situation worse by dating. Or even being friends.

So, for the next two years, they had pretty much steered clear of each other, seeing each other only occasionally and by accident. Until the afternoon almost a month ago when Maggie had realized her increasingly severe physical symptoms were not going to go away, and that she had to do something about her physical problem fast. So she had called Gabe, and instead of returning her phone call, he had dropped by her beach house in person to hear her dilemma and offer his professional medical advice.

One thing had led to another. The next thing she had known, she had been weeping in his arms, and then they were kissing. Nearly three weeks later, Maggie was still thinking about that breathtaking kiss. For no one—*no one*—had ever made her feel like that. Nor did she think anyone else ever would. Which was, bottom line, exactly what had brought her to the decision she had made. She wasn't going to marry anyone if she didn't love him the way she should. And the only person she could envision ever falling in love with was Gabe Deveraux.

Unfortunately, Gabe did not feel the same.

Although he had recently professed a desire to date her again, she suspected that his urge was grounded in her recent troubles and would fade as soon as she landed on her feet. Then, as always, he would be off to rescue the next damsel in distress that came his way.

Maggie had been dumped by Gabe once, albeit for the noblest of reasons—his brother's feelings, and Deveraux family unity. She wasn't setting herself up to get dumped again.

Not that Gabe realized, even subliminally, that's what he was doing. No, she was pretty sure he just looked at each problem—or damsel—as they came into his life, and then acted from his heart, without even thinking about the future. But it was the future, and her baby's future, that Maggie was concerned with now. And in that sense, she knew, Gabe could assist her, the same way he had recently assisted her in finding a specialist to diagnose her medical problems.

"Well, I could use your medical knowledge," Maggie reluctantly conceded, after a moment.

Gabe looked satisfied. "Then let's go through the books together," he said.

A few minutes later, they were in a cozy room, with a round table and two chairs. They sat shoulder to shoulder, elbows on the table, as they pored over each page. "Here's a good one," Maggie said. "The guy is six-four, 220 pounds, with blond hair and blue eyes."

"He also has a history of arthritis in his extended family," Gabe pointed out.

"Okay, what about this one?" Maggie moved on to the next possibility. "Five-eleven, brown hair, green eyes. College-educated."

"He has an aunt on his mother's side who died of breast cancer."

Maggie threw her hands up in exasperation. "Well, everyone is going to have relatives who died of something!"

Gabe leaned back in his chair and folded his arms against his chest. "It would be different if you were talking about marrying someone you were in love with," he explained patiently. "Of course then you would just take your chances and hope for the best. But since you are doing this methodically and you do have a choice, you want to steer away from anyone who has a history of illnesses that can be inherited.''

''Fine.'' Maggie flipped through more pages, wishing she could disagree with him, knowing she couldn't, because everything he said made too much sense. Eventually, she sighed, leaned back and said, ''How do we even know these people are being truthful, anyway?''

''Beats me.'' Gabe shrugged his broad shoulders restively as his gaze meshed with hers. ''I suppose you're taking it on faith that they fill out the forms accurately. I mean, as conscientious as the people here at the fertility clinic are, they can't personally look into the family health backgrounds of each donor.''

''There would be privacy concerns—''

''As well as prohibitive costs.''

''So there could be things that aren't on the list,'' Maggie theorized, worried.

''Probably,'' Gabe agreed seriously. ''Either because a candidate doesn't know about a relative's medical history. Or because he feels he would be disqualified from being a donor if the truth were known.''

Maggie swallowed as the implications of that sank in, beginning to feel a little sick at the idea that she might be trying to bring a child into the world who was destined—because of heredity—to suffer from some terrible disease. "You're not making me feel any better here, Gabe," she said.

Gabe refused to back down, despite her nervousness. "You brought it up. Besides," he regarded her steadily, "I thought you wanted me here to assess the situation—medically speaking."

Actually, Maggie thought, she hadn't wanted him here at all, because his presence was making her have doubts. And yet, because of the seriousness of the situation, she couldn't ignore what he was saying, either. Not when the fate of her as-yet-to-be-conceived child hung in the balance.

The nurse knocked and popped her head in. "Settle on one yet?" she asked with a smile.

"No," Maggie said.

"Not even close," Gabe added.

"Well, that's too bad," the nurse said, glancing at her watch. "Because we were supposed to close up five minutes ago. I hate to ask you to come back, but—my son is playing in a soccer game at five-thirty and I'm in a hurry to close up."

"No problem," Gabe said, already rising.

Easy for you to say, Maggie thought darkly, as she closed the book and stood.

"You can make another appointment on the way out," the nurse hastened to add.

With Gabe watching her, Maggie did.

They walked out into the parking lot. "Where to

now?'' Gabe asked casually, looking once again as if he were about to ask her out on another date.

Deciding that that was the last thing they needed after the unsatisfactory appointment she had just suffered through, Maggie focused on her old standby: her work. ''I don't know about you,'' Maggie said with a smile, ''but I'm going out to your beach house. I want to see how the debris removal is coming.''

Gabe followed her in his sports car. It was nearly six by the time they arrived. Luis, Manuel and Enrico had already knocked off for the day. But their work was complete. All the burned material and the damaged cabinets had been torn out. The kitchen was ready for rebuilding.

''It looks like they even took out all the wiring,'' Gabe said.

Maggie propped both hands on her hips as she continued to look around. ''They have to, for safety's sake.'' She slanted Gabe a glance over her shoulder. ''I assume you want everything built back pretty much the way it was.''

Gabe strolled the length of the downstairs, stroking the rugged line of his jaw, with the backs of his fingers as he moved. ''Actually I thought I'd like to take the opportunity to tear down the wall between the kitchen and the living room and just open it up.''

That was a pretty expensive and time-consuming change, more than Maggie had bargained on. She frowned. ''It'll take a lot longer and be a lot more expensive,'' Maggie warned, hoping he'd change his mind.

No such luck.

Gabe drifted near. "I don't mind," he told her lazily, studying her upturned face.

"Spending time with me?" Maggie tilted her head back and sized him up with a considering look of her own, wondering what the ultimate Good Samaritan was up to now. Had he planned this extra request, or was he just winging it, asking to make things much more complicated, on a whim? "Or the extra construction mess?"

"Both," Gabe said curtly.

Maggie fell silent as she studied the half-hidden apology in his eyes.

She turned away from him, trying not to think about how handsome he looked in his sage-green shirt, coordinating tie and khaki slacks. "You don't owe me anything, Gabe." Least of all this.

"Maybe I think I do."

Maggie turned back in time to see the flicker of guilt in Gabe's expression. It didn't take a genius to know where it had originated. "You've been talking to Enrico, Luis and Manuel, haven't you?" She had known better than to leave the four men alone. Especially since the three Chavez brothers had never forgiven Gabe for his part in her breakup with Chase.

Gabe shrugged, obviously respecting her too much to try and tell her otherwise. "The guys are right," he said quietly. "If not for me, you would be married and have a baby by now."

Maggie rolled her eyes and thrust her hands in the pockets of her jeans. "They're hopelessly overprotective of me. They always have been, and it's gotten worse since my mom and dad died."

"They want you to have it all." Gabe closed the distance between them in three long strides. "Not just a child."

Maggie studied the scuffed toes of her dark-brown work boots. "Suppose that's not possible?"

"Suppose it is?" Gabe put his hands on her shoulders and kept them there. "At least take another few days to think about this."

Heart racing, mouth dry, Maggie looked up at him. "I can't," she said, doing her best not to tremble at his touch.

"Why not?" Gabe asked, so gently she wanted to cry.

Maggie drew a deep breath, extricated herself gracefully from his light, detaining grip and wheeled away. "Because my monthly ovulation window is in three to five days," she told him grimly as she paced back and forth. "And, given the fact my endometriosis has already made me damn near infertile and I may not conceive on the first try, I can't afford to waste any time."

Gabe's eyes darkened with emotion. "I understand all that," he told her quietly.

Maggie squared off with him contentiously. "But?"

"I still don't like the idea of you using an anonymous donor."

"Why not?" At his firm insistence, it was all Maggie could do not to clench her teeth.

"Because I think you should know your baby's father."

So did Maggie, if the truth be known. But that wasn't possible, either, she thought. Furthermore, Gabe should know it, too, instead of pretending otherwise. She shook her head and asked wryly, "And what guy would say yes to a request like that?"

Gabe angled a thumb at his chest. "Me."

FOR A MOMENT, both of them were silent, Gabe every bit as speechless and stunned by his impetuous offer as Maggie looked. Finally, she pulled herself together, shoved a hand through her wavy hair and regaled him with the fiery Irish temperament she had inherited from her dad. "Look, Gabe, I think it's great that you are the Good Samaritan of Charleston, South Carolina, always volunteering to help women out, but this is just too much!"

Gabe drank in the husky vehemence of her voice and the bloom of new color in her fair cheeks, as a car pulled up outside. "So you won't even consider it?" He was stunned by the intensity of his disappointment. Since when had he considered fatherhood?

he wondered in shocked amazement. Never mind with a woman who generally speaking wouldn't give him the time of day! And yet, the thought of Maggie having a baby with someone else—anyone else—even someone anonymous who meant nothing at all to her was even worse. Gabe couldn't say why he felt the way he did, he just knew he didn't want Maggie Callaway to be having anyone's baby but his. End of story.

"For you to be the sperm donor of my baby?" Maggie gaped at Gabe, as a younger woman got out of the car and made her way toward the house. "I hardly think so!" she said vehemently.

"I have to tell you," Daisy Templeton said, as she strolled casually in to join them. "But I have to go with Maggie there. Having a baby via artificial insemination is not the way to go."

Not the opinion Gabe would've expected from Charleston society's wild child and most sought after new photographer. The twenty-three-year-old heiress had been kicked out of seven colleges in five years. Now, Daisy was telling everyone she had no intention of ever going back, and was instead going to devote herself to becoming a professional photographer. Fortunately for the spirited and beautiful young heiress, she had the talent, if perhaps not the discipline, to make her boast a reality, Gabe thought.

"As it happens," Maggie said stiffly, turning to

face Daisy, "in my opinion, artificial insemination of donor sperm is *exactly* the way to go."

Daisy raised her pale blond brows in inquiry, looked at Gabe, then Maggie. "Are you planning to tell the baby who his or her father is?" she asked Maggie carefully.

Maggie shrugged and looked, Gabe noted, even more defensive in light of Daisy's disapproval. "Probably not," Maggie said.

Daisy popped her gum and got her camera out of the case. "Big mistake," Daisy said, shooting Maggie a sober glance. "And I mean gargantuan. I should know because I'm adopted."

That stopped Maggie in her tracks, Gabe noted.

"You have no idea who your parents are?" Maggie asked.

Daisy shrugged as she set up to take the Before pictures for Chase's magazine, *Modern Man*. "No, I don't," Daisy admitted with a troubled look, as she loaded film into her camera, "although I'm working on finding that out."

"It was a problem for you?" Maggie asked.

"More than that," Daisy admitted as she got down on one knee to photograph the burned-out shell of the kitchen. "It was a never-ending source of shame and mystery, frustration and unhappiness."

This surprised Gabe.

"Why?" Gabe asked, brow furrowing as he struggled to understand. Daisy had been adopted by one of Charleston's wealthiest families and had grown up in a privileged home.

Daisy bit her lower lip and looked even more distressed as she related, "Because there had to be some reason for my parents to give me up. And I wondered why my parents abandoned me. My birth mother obviously wanted to carry me to term, but what about my birth father? Why did he walk out on my birth mother or even allow my birth mother to give me up for adoption? I've always wondered why my father didn't love me. And just who the heck is he, anyway? Was he some terrible person or just plain selfish? Did he even know about me? Did my birth mother tell him she was pregnant or did she have me and give me up in secret?"

Good questions, Gabe thought. And ones he had no answers for.

"She must have loved you if she gave you up for adoption," Maggie said gently, doing her best to comfort Daisy.

"I've always told myself that was the case," Daisy said sadly, as she got slowly to her feet and walked to the opposite side of the room, to shoot photos from another angle. "But deep down I wonder if it's true," Daisy continued sadly, "if my birth mother ever really cared about me at all. The bottom line here is that it's a terrible thing for a child to have to grow up knowing that there's something weird or different or secret about the circumstances of his or her birth.

And if you have a choice, as you two clearly do now, you shouldn't do anything to bring a child into the world that you wouldn't want the child eventually to know about.''

"I HAD NO IDEA Daisy was that deep,'' Gabe mused, after Daisy Templeton had finished taking her photos and driven off once again.

"I didn't either,'' Maggie said. She sat down on the steps looking out over the ocean and glumly plucked at the stone-washed fabric of her jeans. "As much as I hate to admit it, she had a point. I mean, how is my baby going to feel when he's old enough to learn his birth father is just a stranger from a sperm bank?''

Gabe sighed as he walked over and settled beside her on the steps. "Probably not very good,'' he said, trying hard not to think about the way her yellow shirt molded the soft, sexy curves of her breasts.

She brought her legs up and wrapped her arms around her bent legs. Resting her head on her knees, she turned her face to look at him and said in a low voice laced with remorse, "I'm not sure that it would be any better to accept a sperm donation from you as a friend, either, though.''

Gabe was silent. Thinking Maggie needed more comfort than she realized, he curved his arm around her shoulders and returned, just as soberly, "I'd hate it if our kid were embarrassed at how he or she had come into this world, or at me or you for our parts in it.''

Maggie drew a deep breath and slowly let it out. ''And now that I think about it, I can't see a child who was old enough to understand the clinical procedure involved in artificial insemination thinking of our decision to procreate with anything but embarrassment and loathing,'' Maggie said.

Gabe nodded and admitted just as freely, ''The last thing a kid wants is to be different from everybody else. It's one thing when there's no helping it. But when you can help it....'' He stopped, shook his head at the emotion welling up inside him. ''Daisy's right,'' he concurred in a low, choked voice as he looked deep into Maggie's light-green eyes. ''It isn't fair.''

''So what am I going to do?'' Maggie asked unhappily, burying her face in her hands.

Gabe, in an attempt to comfort her, rubbed some of the tension from her slender shoulders. ''You could always go the conventional route and get married,'' he said as he massaged his way down her spine.

Maggie bounded to her feet and dashed the rest of the way down the steps. She shoved both hands in the pockets of her jeans and stared at the constantly shifting ocean. Her lips set in a stubborn pout. ''I can't marry someone just because he lusts after me.'' She turned and shot him an angry look over her shoulder. "I almost did that with your brother Chase and look what happened."

Without warning, jealousy stabbed his heart. Gabe swallowed, stood, and followed her down to the bottom of the steps. "Was that what was between the two of you?" he asked, squaring off with her and finding he really needed—wanted—to know. "Lust?"

At his bluntness, Maggie's cheeks flooded with embarrassed color. She turned her eyes away evasively, kicked at the sand with the toe of her work boot. "Let's just say your older brother knows how to court a woman aggressively," she said gruffly. "And there isn't a woman on this earth who doesn't want to be hotly pursued."

Was that where he'd made his big mistake? Not pursuing Maggie aggressively enough?

Suddenly, Gabe knew he couldn't let Maggie get away again. Not when her biological clock was ticking, and she wanted a baby. "Look, this doesn't have to be this complicated," he said urgently, wishing like heck she weren't behaving in a way that made her vulnerable. And whether Maggie realized it or not, her actions were putting her in a place where she was very much at risk of being hurt or taken advantage of. Now, later, it didn't really matter. All he knew was that he was determined not to see that happen.

Maggie lifted her brow. "It doesn't?"

"No, it doesn't," Gabe said firmly, as the solution

to her problem quickly became evident to him. "Because I'll marry you and give you the baby you want via artificial insemination." In fact, the more he thought about it, the more he knew it was the right path to take.

Maggie blinked at him in surprise. "Why would you do that?" she demanded hoarsely, as all the color drained from her face.

"Because Daisy's right." Afraid she was going to bolt if he didn't hang on to her, Gabe took both her hands in his. Wanting her to know how serious he was, he looked deep into her eyes. "If you are going to do this, you should go about it the right and proper way. And I want to help you." More than he had ever wanted to help anyone in his life!

"But we don't love each other," Maggie protested, twin spots of delicate pink color staining her cheeks.

Gabe shrugged off her worries. "That doesn't really matter, given the way you're going to get pregnant," he said, finding the idea of her having artificial insemination was not nearly as repugnant to him if it was with his sperm. "What will matter," Gabe emphasized bluntly now that he had her full attention, "is that we will be officially married when you are getting pregnant and having the baby."

Maggie took a half step back but then gripped his hands all the tighter. "And then what?" she demanded in a soft, wary voice that sent shivers across his skin.

"When the time is right, later," Gabe soothed, knowing it was the only practical solution as well as what Maggie wanted to hear, "we'll divorce."

Maggie looked even more amazed. "And you think it's a workable plan?"

Gabe nodded confidently. "The most workable one so far." He leaned toward her urgently, not stopping until he was close enough to inhale the intoxicating hyacinth fragrance of her skin. "Think about it, Maggie. This way our baby will know who both his or her parents are. I only have one stipulation."

"And that is—?" The hesitation in her eyes was back.

"That I be allowed to be the baby's father while he or she is growing up and that the baby be brought up as a Deveraux as well as a Callaway," Gabe said firmly, knowing he was right about this. "Because every baby deserves both a father and a mother and if possible a loving extended family."

Maggie swallowed. "Well, I can't give my baby that on my own, so…all right," she conceded eventually. "I'll do this your way."

Silence fell between them once again. Maggie furrowed her brow.

"What?" Gabe prodded.

Maggie frowned, stepped back, let go of his hands. "I can't help but think that your family is not likely to approve of this plan of ours," she said worriedly. "Nor are those close to me."

Wishing he could just forget the clinical approach and make love to her, and impregnate her with his seed that way, Gabe shrugged off her concerns. He knew they could work out whatever problems came up. The important thing was that Maggie not go off half-cocked and have some stranger's baby, and then spend the rest of her life—and her baby's, too—regretting it. "They don't even have to know the details," Gabe argued resolutely. "We'll tell them that you're pregnant later, after we've already been secretly married for a few months. That way," he reasoned, "we'll likely get a lot less grief, since people are less inclined to weigh in about a fait accompli."

"All right," Maggie said tremulously. Her chest rose and fell as she breathed in deeply and then released an enormous sigh of relief. "I agree." She shot him a stern, warning glance. "But with my ovulation window ready to hit by the end of the week, we don't have much time."

Chapter Three

"You may kiss the bride," the Sunset Beach justice of the peace said, as soon as Gabe and Maggie had finished their vows.

Gabe turned to Maggie. She was wearing a simple white cotton dress that left her shoulders bare and ended just above her knees, and made her look both surprisingly fragile and very beautiful. At the insistence of the couple presiding over their wedding vows, she had tucked a white rose into her wavy honey-blond hair in lieu of a veil or hat. The overall affect was simple and understated—she made a very lovely bride.

They had decided to get married out on the beach, next to the ocean, rather than inside, in the intimate little chapel, but Gabe wasn't sure this was much better. He still felt as if they *were* married as he leaned forward, looked into her light-green eyes, and delivered a light, gentle kiss to her cheek, even though he knew that in spirit they definitely were not. That this was just a formality done for propriety and their child's sake.

Maggie smiled, stepped back and, looking as eager to end the event as he, thanked the young couple for fitting them in on such short notice. Still clutching the bouquet of silk flowers that had come with the Basic Wedding Package she headed with Gabe to the car.

"Want to have dinner on the way home?" Gabe asked, as they trudged through the sandy dunes and blowing sea grass that separated the ocean from the wedding chapel parking lot.

Maggie's forehead creased as she glanced at her watch. "Maybe we just could hit a drive-through on the way and grab some sandwiches," she suggested instead, "since we have a two-hour drive ahead of us back to Charleston."

"Okay," Gabe did his best to curtail his disappointment as he held her door and watched her settle gracefully into the passenger seat of his sports car.

He supposed that was what he got for having agreed to get married in North Carolina, instead of the state in which they lived. But given the fact that South Carolina had a twenty-four-hour waiting period—and North Carolina had none—and they didn't want anyone besides themselves to know about their hasty wedding just yet, there had really been no alternative. To get married before her monthly ovulation window opened, and/or one of them changed their mind, they'd had to drive north to the quaint

little coastal community, apply for a wedding license
before the county records office closed for the day
and then find a chapel to fit them in before they drove
back.

Now, the deed done, the plain gold wedding bands
on their fingers, they were officially man and wife.

MARRIED, Maggie thought, as she took off the plain
gold band and dropped it into the zipper compartment
in her purse. She was married to Gabe Deveraux.

In name only, of course.

But still, she thought as she rubbed the place on
her finger where the wedding band had been, she was
no longer the free woman she had been just a few
hours ago.

Nor was she really his wife.

They were just…friends.

Casual friends, she reminded herself fiercely, who
were going to have a baby together as soon as they
could get her pregnant the newfangled way. All that
would involve be plastic cups and syringes and
hospital gowns and feet in stirrups.

There would be no champagne, no roses, no romantic dinners for two. So why, she wondered, as
Gabe turned his car into a fast-food restaurant with a
drive-through lane, were her palms all sweaty and her
heart in an uproar? It wasn't as if the vows they had
just said *meant* anything. Noticing she had taken her
ring off, Gabe removed his wedding band, too, and

shoved it in the pocket of his starched white dress shirt.

Abruptly looking as if he felt as uncomfortable and ill at ease as she did sitting side by side in his small sports car, Gabe held the wheel with one hand and loosened his navy and khaki tie and undid the top button on his shirt with his other. He braked as they reached the microphone, then turned to her, a bit impatiently. "What would you like?"

Maggie scanned the menu and tried not to think how awkward this all was. Neither of them had been nearly this tense on the way to get married. "I'll have a chicken sandwich, fries and a lemonade," she said quietly.

Gabe ordered that for her, and a burger meal for himself.

As he drove around to the first window, Maggie reached for her purse.

Gabe held up a hand before she could get out her wallet. "I've got it," he stated firmly as he pulled cash out of the pocket of his khaki trousers. Two minutes later he turned back onto Route 17. "Open mine for me, would you, please?" he said.

Grateful for something to do besides look at Gabe and notice how handsome he was, Maggie flipped open the box, then looked at the thickness of the sandwich inside. Two patties, two slices of cheese, lettuce, pickles, onions and catsup.

Gabe caught her frown and glanced down. "Probably not the smartest thing to be eating while I'm driving, is it?'' he observed with a beleaguered sigh.

Maggie shrugged, knowing it didn't have to be a problem if they didn't want it to be. ''We could stop,'' she suggested.

''No.'' Gabe's jaw was set. ''I can do it. Just hand it to me, would you?''

Maggie knew a man with his mind made up when she saw one. Her father had often had that very look on his face when he'd made a bad decision and decided to soldier through and stick to it nevertheless. ''Okay,'' she said, just as agreeably. She picked the sandwich out of its little brown box.

''Just squish it together some so it's a little flatter,'' Gabe directed.

Maggie kept her skepticism to herself and did as directed. ''I don't know about this,'' she hedged. The sandwich looked and smelled delicious, but the eating of it threatened to be awfully messy.

''It'll be fine,'' Gabe said, taking the sandwich.

One bite later, the first glob of catsup hit his thigh.

''Don't worry about it,'' Gabe said stubbornly, as he continued to eat and drive.

''Okay,'' Maggie said, wondering what it was about men in general that made them have to do things their way, even if it was clearly the wrong way. ''It's your clothing. But at least let me put a napkin or two underneath.''

She opened one up all the way and, being very

careful not to touch his thigh, laid it across the leg of his tailored khaki dress slacks. The napkin slid to the floor the next time he braked, along with the two bits of lettuce he had dropped.

Maggie put down her own sandwich long enough to add another napkin, but this one she tried to angle around his well-muscled thigh so it wouldn't slide off. Unfortunately, that had her touching him, ever so slightly, for about two milliseconds. If one discounted the slight tensing of his facial muscles, he didn't seem to mind.

In a rather moody silence, he finished his sandwich. She finished hers—a lot more neatly since she was able to use both hands. As they worked on their drinks and fries the silence continued to stretch out between them, and Maggie wished she had taken him up on his offer to have a quiet dinner together somewhere on the way back to Charleston, but it was too late for that. And meantime, it looked like that one glob of catsup was really sinking into the fabric of his trousers, despite Gabe's half-hearted effort to dab it off with a crumpled napkin.

"You need some water on that stain," Maggie said.

"Don't have any," Gabe said. Keeping his eyes firmly on the road, he pulled his tie even looser and unfastened another button on his shirt.

"I think I do." Maggie rummaged in her purse and came up with a small bottle of water. She took an unused napkin, wet it, and was about to hand it over when Gabe frowned all the more.

"I really don't want to mess with that, Maggie."

Maggie eyed the spreading orange stain and warned right back. "If you don't get it off before it dries, you could ruin those slacks." She saw no reason to let his male pride be the cause of that.

"Then you do it," he ordered with a disgruntled frown. "Otherwise, just let it be, and I'll take it to the dry cleaners when I get home."

And forever remember their wedding night as the night he also ruined a perfectly good pair of dress pants? Maggie didn't think so.

Frowning too, she added a little more water to the napkin, leaned over and pressed the damp cloth to the orange stain on his trousers. Saw it dim somewhat, as she carefully dampened and blotted, and knew that one more good effort on her part would probably keep his pants from being ruined forever.

She was just about to take care of it when Gabe turned suddenly into a church's vacant parking lot, brought his sports car to a quick stop, and caught her wrist in his hand. "Stop," he commanded fiercely.

And looking down, Maggie saw why.

NOT EXACTLY the way he'd thought he would get aroused on his wedding night, Gabe thought. But here he was, with a hard-on to rival any he had ever had. And Maggie sitting beside him, looking as pale and stricken as any virgin bride about to be led to the bedchambers of a husband she barely knew.

Only they weren't going to consummate their marriage.

Not the usual way.

And her touching him this way was only reminding him of that.

A riot of pink color flooding into her cheeks, Maggie snatched back her hand. "Oh, Gabe, I'm sorry," she said in a low, trembling voice.

So was Gabe. Because now he knew, if he hadn't before, just how much he desired her. And always had. Even as he saw how truly innocent she was at heart. She might have been engaged to his brother— the magazine editor and authority on modern men and their lives and desires and problems—but Maggie didn't know a damn thing about him and his needs. And given the exceedingly stricken way she was staring at him, probably never would, Gabe thought, his spirits sinking even more.

"Forget it," Gabe said, doing his best to mask his disappointment as he thrust his sports car back into gear and headed back onto the coastal highway.

"I never—"

"I said forget it!" Gabe commanded gruffly as two things happened simultaneously: the outskirts of Charleston came into view, and the cell phone on his dash began to ring.

Glad for the diversion, Gabe took the call, then

turned to Maggie as soon as it ended. "I've got to go straight to the hospital," he told her. "I don't have time to drop you first."

"No problem," Maggie said. She offered him a stiff smile. "I can get a cab."

"Or just come with me," Gabe said on impulse, finding he wasn't as anxious to have their time together end as he'd initially thought. "And see if you can help me find out who Jane Doe is, now that she's awake and talking once again."

TO MAGGIE'S RELIEF, Gabe's mood brightened as he parked in the hospital lot and went from secret-new-husband mode to doctor. Unfortunately, there wasn't anything he could do about the drying stain on his slacks, but Gabe rebuttoned the top of his shirt, fixed his tie and slipped his navy sport coat back on. Determined to look as little like a bride as possible, Maggie removed the flower from her hair and tied the pale blue cardigan sweater she'd brought along just in case it got too cool in the car around her neck. Nevertheless, as she and Gabe made their way through the hospital corridors up to the fourth floor, Maggie caught a few curious glances from some of the nurses. She wasn't sure whether they recognized her as the woman who had once been engaged to Chase Deveraux before getting briefly involved with Gabe, or simply thought she and Gabe were about to go out for the evening. But interest in them was high just the same. And it was speculation, Maggie thought to herself, as they entered the hospital room where Jane Doe was, she could well have done without. She didn't want or need to know how quickly the people who worked with Gabe predicted his relationship with her would be over. Because everyone knew Gabe only hung around until the damsel in distress was no longer in trouble.

Gabe took Maggie's elbow as they neared the room. He leaned down to whisper in her ear. "I'm really interested in your assessment of my patient," he said.

Maggie tingled at the warmth of his breath against the side of her face. "I'm no expert." She had no medical background whatsoever.

"But you're a woman," Gabe said, coming even closer. "And a very easy to talk to woman at that." His eyes caressed her face. "I think our Jane Doe might really warm to you."

Maggie had to admit she would like to help someone in need of assistance herself. She also noted immediately upon entering the corner room that the eighty-something patient was a lovely lady, even in a hospital-issue gown. Her long white hair had been caught in an elegant bun at the back of her neck. She had a delicate, aristocratic bone structure, a petite slender frame and exquisitely manicured hands that—

Maggie was willing to bet—had never seen a dishpan or a toilet-bowl brush.

She was sitting up in bed, her faded sea-blue eyes open wide, her cheeks flushed with fever.

"He's coming to get me, you know," Jane Doe told Gabe and Maggie the moment they walked in the room.

"Who's coming?" Gabe asked, as he took her chart off the holder on the wall next to the door.

Jane Doe smiled serenely and clasped her hands in front of her. "Why, my sweetheart, of course."

"What's his name?" Gabe asked gently, as he discreetly checked her chart.

"Oh, I can't tell you that," Jane Doe said vehemently, as Gabe set the chart down on the end of her hospital bed.

"Why not?" Maggie asked, moving to the opposite side of the bed, so she could be close to the woman and yet out of Gabe's way.

"Because our love is very private," she said seriously, as she looked up at Maggie. "And I wouldn't want anything to happen to it. Besides, I don't really think my mama and papa would approve if they knew what I was doing."

Gabe took the stethoscope out of his pocket and put it in his ears. "How old are you?" Gabe asked, as he listened to the woman's chest.

Jane Doe gave him a reproachful look as Gabe

moved from her front to her back. "A lady never tells her age."

Gabe listened to each of her lungs. "Do you know what day it is?"

"Saturday," Jane Doe claimed triumphantly.

Maggie and Gabe exchanged worried glances over Jane Doe's head. It was Tuesday.

"And the year?" Gabe persisted, as he put his stethoscope away and picked up her chart once again.

"I wish you people would stop asking me that," Jane Doe complained, sighing loudly. "It's 1938, of course."

Gabe nodded agreeably and wrote something on her chart.

"Is my driver coming for me soon?"

Gabe looked up with a charming smile. "We'd love to call him for you, if you would just give us his number," Gabe said.

"No." Jane Doe clammed up again. "I can't do that."

"All right. You just rest now." Gabe patted her arm. "And call the nurses if you need anything."

"All right, doctor." Jane Doe settled back against the pillows and closed her eyes.

"Is she okay?" Maggie asked as soon as she and Gabe slipped from the room.

Gabe frowned as he headed for the nurses' station at the other end of the hall. "I don't like the sound of her lungs. I'm going to order a chest X-ray. She might have pneumonia.''

Even Maggie had been able to tell Jane Doe was running a fever. ''Would that make her confused?''

''It could. The combination of fever and illness can do that, especially to older people. I just wish we could find her family—they must be worried sick about her.''

Maggie nodded. ''What are you going to do?''

''The only thing I can do,'' Gabe sighed wearily. ''Contact the media. I hope they'll come out and do a story on her in time for the eleven o'clock news.''

''SO WHAT'S WRONG with this Jane Doe?'' Lane Stringfield asked Gabe as the two of them met in the reception room of Gabe's office some twenty minutes later. The local TV station manager had arrived ahead of his camera crew and reporter. And Gabe had an idea why. He hadn't come for the story—Lane had staff to do that for him—he had come to talk to Gabe. Probably about his estranged wife.

''She definitely has a sprained ankle. She fell on the sidewalk in the historic district late last night. Someone on Gathering Street found her around four this morning. It looked as if she had been there for some time. She was confused and dehydrated, in considerable pain and shock—and she also seemed to be running a little fever, which may have been what caused her to lose her balance and fall in the first place. We were hoping a day in the hospital and a little sleep would make her lucid, but when she woke up a little while ago she was as confused as ever and has stayed that way. I was brought in to evaluate her. I think she may be developing pneumonia—I've ordered a chest X-ray and other tests to help us make the diagnosis.''

''Is she senile?'' Lane Stringfield asked, still making notes on the small leatherbound pad he had taken out of his coat pocket.

''I don't know,'' Gabe said frankly. ''It wouldn't appear so. Usually senile patients aren't nearly as well-groomed as this lovely lady is. Which makes me and the other doctors and nurses on staff think her confusion is something new. But to properly pinpoint the reason for her confusion we need to know who she is and what her medical history is. Which is where you come in. We simply want to run a brief picture of Jane Doe in her hospital bed and ask anyone with information about who she is to come forward.''

''I gather you've already talked to the residents on Gathering Street.''

''The police have,'' Gabe affirmed seriously. ''No one in the neighborhood knows her.''

''All right. I'll instruct my crew as soon as they get here and supervise the filming of the story. In the meantime, as long as we have a few moments,'' Lane continued, looking straight at Gabe. ''I want you to tell me what's going on with my wife.''

MAGGIE HAD BEEN SITTING quietly waiting for Gabe to be able to take her home until this point, but now she figured she really ought to be going. Not wanting to witness what might be a very delicate and/or embarrassing conversation between the two men, she rose to her feet. Gabe grabbed her hand and tugged her back down beside him on the tweed sofa. "You can stay for this," he said firmly, still holding onto her hand.

Suppose I don't want to stay, Maggie thought rebelliously. But given the grip he had on her, she knew she wouldn't get out of there without a tussle, and there was no reason to indulge in anything that undignified.

"Why was my wife at your beach house Sunday night?" Lane demanded, point-blank, the time for niceties and business obviously over.

Gabe shrugged and looked at Lane as if Penny's presence in Gabe's house overnight were nothing for her husband to be concerned about. "She came over to talk to me."

"With a suitcase in tow," Lane pointed out unhappily.

Gabe spread his hands wide. "She didn't plan to spend the night there. She was going to go to a hotel. But then I got called back to the hospital. She was having trouble finding a hotel room—this being the height of the spring tourist season—so I said she could just stay there."

Lane's dark eyes narrowed. "Are the two of you having an affair?"

"No. In fact, I tried to get her to stay with you, or at least not to do anything rash."

"And?" Briefly, Lane looked hopeful.

Gabe frowned, perplexed. "And all I know is that she got a phone call here at the hospital on Sunday afternoon that seemed to upset her terribly. I saw her crying and asked her if everything was all right, but she didn't want to talk about it. The next thing I knew she showed up on my doorstep, and she told me she had just left you." He paused, looked directly at Lane. "I guess I just assumed if someone was having an affair, it was you."

"No." Lane sighed, looking even more troubled and distressed.

"Then what could have happened?" Gabe asked in shared concern. "Who could have called her at the hospital and upset her so much she started to cry?"

And what, Maggie wondered, could that person have said to Penny that would have caused Penny to pack a bag and walk out on her husband?

Lane shrugged. His broad shoulders slumped in defeat. "I don't know what's going on with her the past couple of days," Lane confessed emotionally. He looked at both Maggie and Gabe plaintively. "I mean, I know she's been really sad about not being able to have a baby, and that infertility can make a woman whose biological clock is already ticking kind of crazy. But I've told her that I love her, that I'd be willing to adopt, or have a baby via test tube or whatever she wants.''

"Maybe you should do that again, then," Gabe said, just as earnestly. "Maybe she's just trying to be selfless in leaving you."

"Maybe." Lane stood. "Thanks. Both for the story tonight, and being a friend to me and Penny."

"Any time," Gabe said.

Lane Stringfield paused at the door, turned back to Gabe. "Listen, I've heard your mom is in town again—apparently for good."

"Right."

Lane forged on hopefully. "Any chance she'd consider hosting a local television show now that she's left the network?"

Gabe shrugged. "I don't know. I gave up trying to predict what my mother would or wouldn't do a long time ago. You'll have to ask her."

"Will do," Lane promised.

Lane left and Gabe turned back to Maggie.

Funny, Maggie thought. She'd thought she had a very good idea who Gabe was—the incessantly selfless Good Samaritan who busied himself helping one person after another. Now, having seen a flash of melancholy and pessimism in his personality as he talked with Lane, she wasn't certain she knew him at all. She studied him openly. "The fact that the Stringfields might divorce really bothers you, doesn't it?"

"Yeah—maybe because I just never saw it coming for the two of them. They've been married for five years now. I've known Penny for just slightly longer. I attended their wedding and have been friends to both of them, and really feel they belong together."

"Then…?" Maggie asked, confused.

Gabe shrugged. "I can't explain Penny's behavior any more than Lane can," he told Maggie bluntly. "All I know for certain is that my own parents separated abruptly without any explanation and then ended up getting divorced. I don't want to see the same thing happen to Penny and Lane, because I think they'd end up regretting it the same way my parents have."

"And yet," Maggie observed quietly, "you took Penny in Sunday night, knowing how it would probably look to Lane and everyone else."

A muscle worked in Gabe's cheek. He looked at Maggie, clearly resenting the implication. "She's a friend. She showed up on my doorstep crying hysterically and telling me her marriage to Lane was over. What was I to do? Throw her out?"

If that would've saved her marriage, Maggie thought, yes, that is exactly what you should have done, Gabe. But out loud, she said only, in a clear, polite tone, "You could have called Lane and heard his side of the story or let him know how upset his wife was and asked him to come over and talk things out with her."

Gabe scowled. "I didn't want to make things any worse. And from the way Penny was acting, I thought Lane might have been cheating on her," he admitted unhappily.

"But you don't think so now," Maggie guessed.

"No." Gabe studied Maggie carefully, obviously wanting her opinion. "Do you?"

"He didn't act like he was," Maggie conceded, just as cautiously, "but then I don't know Lane. Or Penny. So I'm really not equipped to assess their behavior."

Gabe was silent, thinking. He looked at his watch. "I guess I better get you home," he said glumly after a moment.

Maggie nodded. Some wedding night this was turning out to be. Even for an-in-name-only marriage.

Chapter Four

Gabe had just finished rinsing the shampoo out of his hair Wednesday morning when he heard the doorbell. It was followed by pounding. Figuring it was probably the work crew, there to start their workday a little ahead of schedule, Gabe grabbed a towel and wrapped it around his waist. He hurried downstairs to let the Chavez brothers in, dripping water as he went. He was stunned but delighted to see only Maggie on the other side of the threshold. He grinned at her shocked expression, and in an effort to lighten the sudden tension between them, said teasingly, "You rang?"

An embarrassed flush climbed from her neck to her face, making her look all the more beautiful in that sweet and capable way. "I thought you'd be still asleep," she said.

Gabe glanced down at the beads of water glistening on his arms and chest. "Obviously, not." Deciding this was nothing the neighbors needed to see, he motioned Maggie in.

She stepped around him gingerly, looking fiercely independent once again. Her glance roamed the nearly-naked length of him. "You can finish drying off, if you want," she told him coolly.

"I want to hear what was so urgent first."

"Okay." Maggie squared her slender shoulders, drew a deep breath, and looked him straight in the eye. "I called the fertility clinic as soon as it opened at 7:00 a.m. I told them you had agreed to be the donor, and scheduled an appointment for both of us this afternoon."

That was news. *Important* news. Gabe blinked, couldn't help but ask, "Already?"

The self-conscious blush in Maggie's cheeks deepened a little more. "I'm ovulating. I know." She held up a hand before he could protest. "It's several days early, but when I took my temperature this morning, there was no denying I'm ready to go. So they said they would work us in this afternoon at four." She peered at him, somehow managing to appear haughty and anxious at the same time. "You can make it, can't you?" she asked in a low, trembling voice.

Gabe knew it would take quite a bit of rearranging. He had a full day of patients at the hospital ahead of him, many of them critically ill and hence demanding lots of medical attention. But, this was why he had married her—to get her pregnant.

Not, Gabe mused unhappily, that he was looking forward to spilling his seed into a cup. Not when it would have been so much better to do things the old-fashioned way. But making love to Maggie hadn't been part of their agreement. And he was pretty sure, given the way she felt about him, that it wouldn't be in the future, either. "Sure," he said.

Maggie narrowed her eyes at him. "You're not getting cold feet, are you?"

Gabe shifted so he stood with his feet braced farther apart, one hand jammed on his waist, the other holding the towel precariously in place. "Actually, all of me is a little cold," Gabe fibbed, knowing full well that wasn't exactly true, either. There was one part of him that was heating up quite nicely. And Maggie would know it, too, if she let her glance fall past his waist.

Deciding it would be wise to make his exit before that happened and he permanently scared off his new bride, he turned and started for the stairs. "I'm going to get dressed," Gabe said. "Make yourself at home." He returned five minutes later, dressed and ready for work. To his amazement, Maggie was no longer alone. His aunt Winnifred and her longtime butler, Harry, were with her.

"I didn't hear you come in," he told Winnifred and Harry.

"Maggie saw us and let us in before we rang the bell," Winnifred explained.

Maggie smiled, looking a lot more relaxed—probably because they now had two very good chaperones, Gabe thought.

"I figured you'd already had enough doorbell ringing for one morning," Maggie said dryly.

And she probably hadn't wanted him to come down the stairs from the loft half-dressed again, Gabe thought.

It was also clear from the way his aunt was dressed—in the clothes she tended her flower garden in—that she had rushed right over, too. Otherwise, his widowed aunt, who was one of the social doyennes of Charleston, would have taken the time to change into one of the elegant tea dresses she wore when making a daytime social call.

"So what brings you here so early this morning?" Gabe asked his aunt cheerfully. His dad's younger sister was one of his favorite people.

"A story I saw on the local news about that lovely elderly lady admitted to Charleston Hospital night before last," Winnifred said. "I can't quite place her, but she looks very familiar to me."

Finally, they were getting somewhere, Gabe thought, pleased. "You think you've seen our Jane Doe before?" he asked hopefully.

"I'm almost certain of it," Winnifred said as she perched on the edge of Gabe's living-room sofa. "But I just can't place her. And the thought that I might be able to help her find her way back to her family, if only I could figure out who she is, is really frustrating me.''

Gabe guessed there was at least thirty years difference between the two women's ages, since his aunt was fifty and Jane Doe appeared to be in her eighties. So they probably hadn't hung out together. But there were also some similarities. "She does look and talk as if she might be in your social milieu," Gabe said. Both Jane Doe and his aunt Winnifred were lovely and proper very old-fashioned Southern ladies.

"Except if she were," Winnifred disagreed, "I would know who she is. You know how many parties I attend. There isn't a charity or civic board in Charleston of which I am not a member."

Gabe had to admit his long-widowed aunt was extraordinarily well-connected. Since the death of her husband during their first year of marriage some twenty-five years before, Winnifred had thrown herself into her various good causes. "Maybe Jane Doe used to socialize a lot when she was much younger but doesn't any more, which is why you vaguely remember her."

Winnifred mulled that over for a moment. Seeming to agree with the validity of his theory, she asked, "Do you suppose I could speak to her?"

Gabe hesitated. They'd put a No Visitors order on Jane Doe before they ran the news story on her, to protect her from any unscrupulous people who might take advantage of her. "I suppose it would be all right if you didn't stay long and didn't agitate her—particularly if you can help us identify her. But I have to warn you that she has a slight case of pneumonia and she's not feeling well.''

Maggie looked concerned. ''Is she going to be okay?''

Gabe nodded. ''I think so. We started her on IV antibiotics last night and the respiratory therapists were in to work with her, to keep her lungs open. But,'' Gabe turned back to his aunt Winnifred, ''according to the nurses I spoke to this morning, she is still very confused. So you mustn't allow yourself to be upset by anything she says or does.''

''Oh, I won't. I promise.'' Winnifred said. She then turned to Maggie and clasped both of Maggie's hands in hers—a gleam in her eye, her smile suddenly matchmaker-sly. ''So, I never did get around to asking you, Maggie. When exactly did you come back into Gabe's life?''

OUT OF THE MOUTHS of clever women, Maggie thought to herself.

Behind Winnifred, her very proper British butler Harry harrumphed. ''Perhaps we should be going,'' he suggested firmly.

''Not,'' Winnifred turned and shot her handsome employee a look that was far more knowing than usual between an employer and employee, ''until I get some answers to my questions.''

"I'm helping Gabe with the rebuilding of his kitchen," Maggie said, wondering even as she spoke if there was some sort of romance brewing between Gabe's aunt and her long-time employee.

And in return, Maggie continued silently to herself, Gabe is helping me have the baby I—we—both want.

Winnifred turned to Gabe. "Well, this is a switch. Usually you're the one helping the woman out of a crisis. Not the other way around." Winnifred narrowed her eyes at Gabe thoughtfully. "Or is there a crisis here, too?" she asked bluntly.

"Why would you even ask that?" Gabe retorted with uncharacteristic grumpiness. Striding over to the entertainment center housing his stereo, TV and DVD player, he made a great show of straightening his necktie while looking at his reflection in the glass.

"Maybe because you seem to be assisting a different woman out of some sort of calamity every two to three weeks," Winnifred shot back, just as calmly.

Gabe swung around to face the three of them, steam practically rolling out of his nose. "You're exaggerating. Besides, that's not the case now," he told them all flatly.

"Good. Because Eleanor left me a note in my mailbox a few days ago saying if you didn't stop that you would never find the right woman and settle down."

"Eleanor Deveraux, the family ghost?" Maggie cut in, wanting to make sure she was following this correctly.

"Yes," Gabe told Maggie impatiently. "And Eleanor is dead, Aunt Winnifred," Gabe said sternly, letting them all know with a hard glance that he didn't believe in what had come to be known as the Deveraux Family Legacy. The tale had started years ago, when his great-aunt Eleanor Deveraux had fallen in love with Dolly Lancaster's fiancé, sea captain Douglas Nyquist. After being jilted, Dolly had put a curse on Douglas Nyquist—whose ship had sunk off the coast of Charleston in a terrible tropical storm—and on the entire Deveraux family. Eleanor had died within the year, of a bad case of the flu that everyone said was really a broken heart. As a result of "the legacy," until the recent happy marriages of Gabe's brothers, Mitch and Chase, every Deveraux romance or marriage had ended either prematurely or in tragedy. It had reached the point that some in the family—such as Gabe's younger sister Amy—truly felt they had been cursed.

"Ghost or not, she left this note." Aunt Winnifred pulled a faded card from her oversized purse. Gabe looked at it, frowned all the harder, then shoved it back at his aunt, who deliberately ignored his scowl and handed it to Maggie for her perusal.

"The penmanship is beautiful," Maggie murmured as she ran her hand over the beautiful ivory and gold notepaper.

"Isn't it?" Winnifred beamed. "And it matches the card that was left on the deck of the Deveraux yacht the night Chase and Bridgett set off for their honeymoon. The card that predicted that Mitch would be next to get married. And of course he did!''

''That was an arranged courtship!'' Gabe protested.

Winnifred turned to Maggie. ''Did you know Mitch and Lauren stumbled onto Eleanor's secret trysting place?''

''They also found an intruder running in and out of it at all hours of the day and night,'' Gabe said, looking all the more worried. ''At least until they changed the locks.''

Winnifred sighed, her disappointment evident, as she said, ''If Eleanor's old love letters from Captain Nyquist hadn't been stolen from the secret room, we could have compared the penmanship.''

Gabe scowled, his patience with family lore clearly exhausted. ''Forgeries happen all the time. Face it, Aunt Winnifred. Our family is the victim of an elaborate hoax.''

''I DON'T THINK you should have been so hard on her,'' Maggie said, after Winnifred and Harry had left for the hospital.

Gabe's stomach rumbled hungrily. He went to the small refrigerator beneath the bar in the living room and pulled out a carton of milk and a box of wheat flakes he'd brought home the night before. Remembering he had no dishes—they'd all been destroyed in the fire—he shook some cereal into an old-fashioned glass, added milk, and picked up a cocktail spoon from the cutlery set on the bar. He offered it to Maggie. She shook her head. "Thanks. I've already eaten. And I meant what I said about your aunt. She's a wonderful person."

Gabe studied Maggie over the top of his glass. He didn't remember her being so caught up in the specifics of the legend when she had been engaged to Chase. Or this emotional. But maybe that had to do with her ovulating, and thinking today might be the day her—their—baby was made. Gabe had to admit it was a sobering thought. Exciting, but sobering, too.

With effort, Gabe turned his attention away from baby-making with Maggie and the fierce desire he'd already felt for her that morning, and back to the conversation at hand. "Aunt Winnifred is also completely over the top when it comes to our ancestor."

Her slender legs crossed at the knee, Maggie sat forward earnestly on the middle cushion of his sofa. She laced her fingers together and hooked them over one knee. "Perhaps understandably, since both Eleanor Deveraux and Winnifred lost the loves of their lives at very young ages and never loved anyone else."

Gabe took another bite of cereal. "If you can discount Harry," he said.

Maggie tilted her head to the side. As she did so, her wavy blond hair shifted, too, gently caressing one side of her face, falling away from the other. "You

think there may be something going on there, too,"
she presumed.

Gabe shrugged. He knew it wouldn't be proper—
his socialite aunt and her butler. "Harry has been aunt
Winnifred's most intimate confidante for the past ten
years."

Briefly, Maggie looked shocked. "You don't think
they're actually…"

"No," Gabe cut in quickly. Perish the thought! "I
think they both want to but are too proper even to
think about taking their relationship to the next level.
Which is why aunt Winnifred is always projecting her
own romantic fantasies onto the rest of the Deveraux
clan. She wants to enjoy love, but only dares to do
so vicariously."

Maggie knitted her brows as she thought about that.
Finally, she stood. Today she wore good-fitting khaki
cargo pants, a white long-sleeved button-front shirt
and a denim vest.

As Gabe shook more cereal into his glass, she shot
him an unexpectedly flirtatious glance. "Good thing
your aunt doesn't know we're married, then."

Gabe nodded as he topped off his wheat flakes with
more milk. "She'd either think it was for real or that
it was only going to last a few weeks."

"She wouldn't be far wrong." Maggie stepped
closer and stood, both hands on her hips, legs braced
apart, boot-clad feet planted firmly on the floor. She

looked fresh and pretty in the morning light flooding in through the windows.

"We're only going to be together until after the baby is born," Maggie noted practically. "And not publicly until we know I've gotten pregnant."

Gabe tried not to think about how sexy Maggie would be when she was carrying his child. It was hard enough being near her with nothing between them, but a plan and a certificate of marriage.

"I don't think we should tell people that, though," Gabe replied as he drank in the intoxicating hyacinth fragrance of her skin and hair.

"Why not?" she asked curiously.

"Because then they would question the wisdom of our actions."

"The way we are?" Maggie quipped lightly.

Gabe refused to be sidetracked from the serious discussion ahead of them. He finished his cereal and put his glass and spoon aside. "My guess is most of them won't even expect it to last more than a few weeks, in any case."

Maggie narrowed her eyes as she theorized matter-of-factly, "Because of your penchant for playing the Good Samaritan?"

Gabe wasn't about to take any grief—from any-one—about that. Not even Maggie. He knew what he did was vital to those around him. "When I see some-one in trouble, I have to do what I can to assist them," he explained. It was just the way he was.

"And then you lose interest when their problems are solved," Maggie presumed.

Her conclusion rankled. It sounded as if he didn't care, and he did. On the other hand, he couldn't exactly go around wearing his heart on his sleeve and expect to last more than a couple of days. He had learned to keep a certain emotional distance from those he was trying to help while in medical school. That distance kept his thinking clear, his actions grounded. But he wasn't sure Maggie, or anyone else who didn't have a medical background, would understand that.

"It's not even that involved," Gabe said practically as he opened the windows on the first floor to let the fresh ocean breeze in and the still somewhat smokey scent clinging to the interior of his beach house out. "I mean, I know sometimes it looks intense, when I'm in the process of helping a woman solve her problems. But it doesn't feel that way on the inside. On the inside, I'm just trouble-shooting or working toward a solution."

"So when it's over...?" Maggie walked with him from window to window, lending a hand when she could.

Gabe shrugged and, finished with the windows, rested his shoulder against the wall. "Then the person I'm helping and I both feel relief and move on." The person he was helping felt grateful, and he felt the satisfaction he always felt whenever he helped someone, in any capacity. As far as Gabe was concerned, it was a win-win situation.

Maggie peered at him curiously beneath a veil of lashes. "Are you closer afterward?"

"Not the way you mean," Gabe said. Not as if he and the various women he had helped had been emotionally or physically involved, never mind head over heels in love. No, it was a different kind of intimacy, an intimacy born of crisis that was also very specific and narrow and short-lived. But again, he wasn't sure Maggie, with her non-medical background, would understand that. "To tell you the truth, I don't think I've ever been that close to anyone," he said.

"IF YOU'D LIKE to reschedule, we have an appointment at four-fifteen," the fertility clinic nurse told Maggie.

"No. I'm sure he'll be here," Maggie said confidently. *Gabe wouldn't let her down. Not about something this important. Not after he had promised to help her make a baby and had already secretly married her.*

"The thing is," the nurse continued, looking every bit as uneasy as Maggie felt, "we don't have a donation from him yet, and—"

"I'm sure he can do it quickly," Maggie said, crossing her fingers, and praying it was true. "He's a doctor, so he's familiar with medical procedure, and all of that. And he knows I'm ovulating."

The nurse looked even more skeptical.

"If I could just get in a gown, and then wait—" Maggie pleaded, determined to have a baby with Gabe no matter what it took.

The nurse sighed, glanced at her watch, then finally conceded. "Well, all right. But if he's not here by four forty-five—"

"I totally understand," Maggie said, plucking her cell phone from her shoulder bag. She called Gabe. The hospital operator said he had already checked out for the day, but promised to page him on his beeper. Maggie breathed a sigh of relief, and began to undress. Obviously, Gabe was on his way, and had simply been delayed by traffic. She put on the cotton gown and snapped it at the neck, then sat up on the examining table to wait for Gabe's return call, her cell phone cradled expectantly in her hand.

One minute passed. Another. Then five, ten, fifteen. Finally at nearly five o'clock, the nurse came back in.

"Gabe hasn't shown up yet, has he?" Maggie surmised unhappily, knowing the clinic would be closing down for the day momentarily.

The nurse shook her head sadly. "I'm sorry, hon," she said sympathetically. "Maybe he had car trouble or something."

And maybe, Maggie thought furiously, it was something worse. Maybe he had just changed his mind.

Chapter Five

"I'm sorry," Gabe told Maggie shortly after seven that evening.

Maggie shot him a resentful look, trying hard not to notice just how handsome he looked in the sea-blue shirt and tie and coordinating slacks, or how determined he appeared to be to have his own way.

"Well, that much I figured." Deciding she was way underdressed for this confrontation—she had taken a long bubble bath and put on her favorite pair of peach silk pajamas the moment she got home—Maggie started to close the front door in Gabe's face.

He caught the door with his hand, his fingers closing over hers, then paused to search her face like the protector he clearly thought he was. "Aren't you going to at least hear me out?" he demanded impatiently.

Maggie's fingers tingled from the warmth and strength of his even while her stubborn determination to kick him out of her life once and for all grew.

"What's there to say?" she asked in a sweet, sarcastic voice meant to provoke him as much as he had already provoked her. She curled her bare toes on the cool ceramic tile beneath her feet and, refusing to succumb to the seductive fragrance of his aftershave, tilted her face up to his.

Gabe's glance roved the damp tendrils of her hair at the nape of her neck, caressed her lips, before returning with slow deliberation to her eyes. "I got caught up at the hospital and couldn't get away," he told her in a low sexy voice that sent shivers of awareness shimmering over her skin.

Wishing like heck she'd thought to put on a bra, or at least a tank top underneath her pajamas—anything to cover the tightening of her nipples in the cool evening air—Maggie looked him straight in the eye. "I don't believe you," she told him, even more sweetly.

His jaw dropped at her no-holds-barred declaration.

Maggie held up a hand before he could interrupt, with his own version of events. She stepped out onto the porch of her beach house—which, unfortunately, just happened to be along the same stretch of beach as his. "You never wanted to do this," she accused as she propped both her hands on her waist and glared up at him.

Gabe sighed. "You're right. I didn't."

Maggie girded her thighs defiantly, prodding, "Because…?"

Gabe's glance drifted leisurely over her in a frank, sensual appraisal, before returning to her face. He lounged against the railing on her sunporch and continued to search her eyes. "You want to know the truth?"

Wasn't that a loaded question? "Nothing but," Maggie assured him bluntly, over the tumultuous rhythm of her heartbeat.

Gabe shrugged his broad shoulders. Abruptly, his expression was as impassive as his eyes. "It seems like a cold way to bring a baby into the world. It's okay for someone for whom there is no other way. But it seems to me that whenever possible a baby should be made in person, and in love."

Maggie had always felt the same, until her desperation to have a child coupled with the possibility of infertility cancelled out everything else. She crossed her arms in front of her, then asked defiantly, "Then what are you proposing we do?" Despite her efforts, she was unable to quell the hurricane of emotions spiraling through her.

Gabe looked glad she had asked that. He crossed the distance between them, took her into his arms, so they were pressed together length to length, and lowered his glance to hers. "This."

Maggie barely had time to gasp in shock and surprise before Gabe caught her head in his hands, tilted her face up, and then his lips were fastened on hers in a riveting, passionate kiss that literally robbed her of all thought and reason. She melted against him as his tongue swept the inside of her mouth, and he possessed her in a deep, sexy way that took her breath away. The hardness of his chest pressed against the softness of her breasts. Lower still he was even harder, more masculine and insistent. Tremors of arousal swept through her, igniting to flame. Maggie hadn't expected Gabe to want to make love to her in order to make their baby. But now that he was holding her this way, kissing her so passionately, she couldn't imagine him not making her his—even if it was just for a little while. She clutched his shirt, and still kissing him madly all the while, dragged him across the portal into the house. The door shut behind them, and then they were locked together.

"Maggie—" Gabe murmured, as he briefly came up for air.

Whatever he was about to say, Maggie didn't want to hear it, didn't want anything interfering with her ultimate goal of having a baby, someone in her life to love. "No thinking, Gabe," she insisted, just as ardently, as she grasped him by the hand and led him swiftly and irrevocably down the hall, and up the stairs. "No talking," she insisted fiercely. "Just feeling."

Too many things had almost happened and then hadn't, in her life. For too long, she'd been alone. But not anymore, Maggie thought. Not when Gabe was here after all, ready to help, and she was ovulating, their baby about to be made. Still pressing hot, wanton kisses down the slope of his throat, she guided him into her bedroom, and over to the white cottage-style double bed.

Gabe wanted Maggie fiercely as they tumbled onto the tidy mint-green comforter on her bed. But something about the way she was rushing him along, the way she had stopped kissing him as she straddled him and nervously unbuckled his belt, grappled clumsily with his zipper, gave him pause. Maggie was acting like a frightened virgin on a mission to get pregnant, not the confident, sexy, fiercely independent woman he knew.

Like it or not, the relationship between them was turning clinical—and desperate—again. And Gabe couldn't help but compare that with the lusty and fulfilling relationship she'd undoubtedly had with his older brother, Chase. He'd lived in Chase and Mitch's shadows for all of his life—he didn't want to come up last again. Not in the category of making love. And especially not in Maggie's estimation of him, as a man, as a lover, as a friend. And that, Gabe realized reluctantly, as Maggie's silky, warm fingers brushed against his waist, meant he could do only one thing.

He caught her hand before she could draw the metal slide all the way down, held it captive there against his fly. He looked at her firmly. ''This isn't right either,'' he said. He wanted Maggie. Oh, how he wanted her. But not this way. Hurriedly, furtively, and without heart. Because if they did it that way, she'd regret it—and resent him for it later. Maybe not right away, but eventually. And that was a path he wasn't going to take. They'd let too much drive them apart already.

Maggie tensed from head to toe as hot-pink color flooded her face. She laughed shakily and pressed the back of a hand to her soft lips. "I'm not surprised." Bitterness and hurt flooded her face as she withdrew her other hand from his fly, scooted over to the edge of the bed. Light-green eyes radiating despair, she regarded him helplessly. "In fact, I probably should have expected as much." Looking all the more distressed, she shoved a trembling hand through the honey-colored softness of her hair, pushing it away from her face. "This sort of thing always happens to me on my wedding night—or in this case, the delayed-by-one-day wedding night."

Gabe blinked. "What are you talking about?" he demanded, beginning to be as upset as she was about the mess they had once again made of things. "You've never been married before," he said.

"Actually," Maggie retorted, slowly, "I have. Only it was never really legal—so from that standpoint it doesn't count."

"Which is why," Gabe guessed, "you didn't tell the clerk about it when we applied for our marriage license."

"Right."

Knowing this was one story he had to hear, Gabe shifted from a prone to a sitting position and leaned back against the painted white headboard. "So how long ago was this?" he asked.

Maggie swallowed hard, looked deep into Gabe's eyes, and continued, "When I was sixteen, I dated someone my mother and father didn't approve of. And I eloped."

Sixteen! Gabe took a moment to let that sink in, even as his heart went out to her. "That doesn't sound like a very good introduction to lovemaking," he told her sympathetically. Understanding—because he had made his own share of very foolhardy decisions as a teenager.

"Isn't that the truth." She hung her head in shame. "My 'husband,' who was eighteen, was so anxious and guilt-ridden about what we'd done he was unable to perform. Anyway, our parents caught up with us the next day. Because my boyfriend and I had used forged letters of parental permission for me, it was easy to get the marriage annulled. My boyfriend and I were so mortified by what had happened that we never spoke of it or saw each other again. And now here I am 'married' again—for all the wrong reasons—and my husband is unable to perform." Maggie stood, clasped her hands together in front of her. "Maybe the universe is trying to tell me something." She turned away from him and released a troubled sigh.

"Like what?" Gabe demanded, almost afraid to hear the answer, given the tension in her feminine, five-foot-five frame.

Maggie swung back around to face him and looked him straight in the eye. She clamped her lips together as if she were not going to allow herself to continue. Then to his chagrin, she did anyway.

"Like we should end this travesty of a marriage *now,* Gabe," she stated in a low, excessively stubborn tone. "Before we further humiliate ourselves or anyone else finds out about it."

"OKAY, SO WHAT'S the emergency?" Jack Granger asked Gabe the next morning when they met for a run before breakfast.

Gabe knew if anyone could help him figure out what to do next, it would be Jack, who was not only a trusted friend and former college roommate, but an attorney for Deveraux Shipping Company. On the other hand, Gabe decided on the spur of the moment, there was no need to humiliate himself unnecessarily.

"A friend of mine has a problem," Gabe fibbed as they jogged down the beach, making tracks in the sand.

"Okay, shoot," Jack said affably.

Deciding they were taking it way too easy, Gabe took a deep breath of the salty ocean breeze and picked up his speed. "He wants to know how he can stay in a secret marriage not yet consummated when his bride wants out.''

Jack shrugged off-handedly as he easily kept pace with Gabe. ''Do what the politicians do. Delay, delay, delay. And hope that whatever objection there is will sort of fade away in the meantime.''

Gabe grimaced in remorse. Unfortunately, he didn't think Maggie would soon forget the way he had stopped making love to her. Especially when it so closely mirrored the way he had come on to her, and then decided it would be best if they didn't date each other after all, two years ago.

Jack continued to study Gabe thoughtfully as they raced along the dunes. ''By the way,'' Jack continued sagely as they ran single file through a hedge of waist-high sea grass waving in the breeze, and over several uneven hills of sand along a particularly narrow section of beach, ''your friend who's keeping this a secret—if he's prominent,'' Jack warned, ''and the marriage record is published anywhere within the state or general geographic area, your friend can bet his marriage won't stay secret for long.''

Too late, Gabe realized he and Maggie should have gone a lot farther away than Sunset Beach, North Carolina, to be married, but he couldn't worry about that now. He had to worry about Maggie and their marriage and the mistakes he had made.

Deciding to buy himself time any way he could,

Gabe parted company with Jack and jogged back to the beach house.

As Gabe had hoped, Maggie was there with her crew instructing them on how to rebuild the kitchen exactly the way it had been before the fire. Which was something, Gabe thought, that could be accomplished much too quickly. Particularly for a guy trying to buy time.

"Hold it," Gabe said, as he raced up to joined them. He stood next to Maggie, dripping sweat onto the deck. Grabbing a towel off the rail, he blotted his face and head, before draping it around his neck. "I don't want the kitchen exactly the way it was before."

If possible, Maggie looked even less pleased to see him. "I thought you said you weren't interested in a new design," she reminded briskly.

Gabe ignored the equally tenacious expressions on the faces of Luis, Manuel and Enrico Chavez. "That was before I thought about it," he announced cheerfully, warmed by the idea of how much time—and opportunity to be with Maggie—an undertaking like this might require. "Now I've thought about it," he continued confidently, folding his arms across his chest, "and I want a lot bigger kitchen that opens up onto the living room."

Maggie spun around on her heel and stalked back into his house, leaving him to follow at will. "That means we'll have to take down this wall." She pointed to the barrier between the two rooms.

Gabe shrugged as Enrico, Luis and Manuel took their places behind Maggie. The trio looked like angry sentries, ready to demolish him at will, Gabe thought. And although he liked the idea of Maggie being protected by her three employees, he did not cotton to the notion of them putting up interference between him and Maggie. Steadfastly ignoring Maggie's bodyguards, Gabe smiled at Maggie pleasantly. "Fine by me."

Maggie appeared to be hanging on to her temper with a great deal of effort. "We've already started rebuilding this wall," she explained with exaggerated patience, pointing to the brand-new drywall that had just been nailed into place.

Gabe couldn't have cared less what had to be done or undone, just so he could keep Maggie in his life as long as possible. "So I'll eat the extra cost," he said. He didn't use his trust fund anyway.

Luis stepped forward, looked at Gabe, then turned to Maggie. "You know, you don't have to do this job," he pointed out respectfully. "We have plenty of work."

Maggie stared at Gabe, no cooler in temper than she had been the night before when she had summarily "ended" their secret marriage and thrown him out of her beach house. "I'm not afraid of difficult clients," Maggie announced sweetly, to one and all.

She planted her hands on her hips and stepped forward until she stood toe-to-toe with Gabe. Angling her head up at him, she finished with exaggerated cordiality, "Especially when they pay through the nose for all their stupid decisions."

Liking the fire in Maggie's eyes—for fire meant passion, and passion meant she had feelings for him, even if they weren't exactly the kind he wanted—Gabe turned to their audience. Trying not to notice how very much they wanted to beat him to a pulp, he grinned and continued as cheerfully as ever, "See, fellas?" Gabe spread his hands wide on either side of him. "She's up to the challenge."

Enrico stepped forward. He angled a beefy thumb at his chest. "Maybe we do not think that is wise."

"I'm the boss, here, guys," Maggie interrupted, just as evenly, as she once again put herself between Gabe and the crew. She looked at the Chavez brothers sternly, as her fiercely independent streak became prominent once again. "I'll decide what jobs we take and what jobs we don't. And we're finishing this one no matter how much it costs *him*."

Glad that was settled, Gabe rubbed his hands together. "Okay. Great. So when and how do we start?"

Maggie sighed. Loudly. "If you want a new design—" she began, without a great deal of patience.

"I do."

"—then we have to meet to draw it up," Maggie

explained, tapping one booted foot against the newly laid plywood subflooring.

"I can do it as soon as I shower," Gabe said.

She gave him a look—no doubt remembering his no-show of the afternoon before.

"I've got the day off," Gabe explained.

"Fine," Maggie said curtly. She turned to her crew. "You guys might as well take the day off, too, and spend it with your families since it looks like we'll have to work through at least part of the weekend to make up for this."

Enrico nodded. "All right."

Luis harrumphed. "You call us if you need us."

"We can be here in no time flat," Manuel promised.

"WELL, WHAT DO YOU KNOW, you actually showed," Maggie said as she let Gabe into the design studio at the rear of her house. The room sported floor-to-ceiling windows, and overlooked the Atlantic Ocean. During hurricane season, when a storm was on its way, the windows had to be boarded up, but the rest of the time they were unadorned, and let in a plethora of dazzling golden sunlight and Carolina-blue sky that seemed the perfect showcase for Maggie's exemplary talent.

"Of course I showed." Gabe was insulted that his wife seemed to have half expected he might have done otherwise. He'd never been a rude or inconsiderate person. He didn't think he was one now, either.

Maggie lifted her slender shoulders in an indifferent shrug. "You didn't yesterday afternoon," Maggie pointed out with a censuring frown.

"I made up for that by catching up with you last night," Gabe countered, defending his tardiness as they sat down, side by side, at her drawing table. When was she going to realize he had married her to help—not hurt—her? he wondered, upset.

"I don't know about making up for it, but you certainly made some things clear," Maggie said. "Like the fact that you and I don't have any business creating a child together after all. And that being the case, I think we should get the marriage annulled."

Although Maggie hadn't actually said as much last night, after their disastrous bout of near-lovemaking, Gabe had seen the look in her eyes as she threw him out of her house and had known that this statement was coming. Hence, his preemptive strike/early-morning conversation with his friend and attorney Jack Granger.

"Two annulments?" He regarded her steadily, unable not to note how pretty—and businesslike and off-putting—she looked in jeans, a long-sleeved pink oxford cloth shirt, and a navy blazer. Even her dark-brown work boots had acquired a new sheen that indicated they had been recently cleaned. "Come on, Maggie. You don't want to do that."

Maggie gave him a smile that was lethal enough to rip out his heart. "If you think I don't," she said, "then you don't know me at all."

Silence fell between them. Gabe swallowed and cautioned himself not to move too fast. He didn't want to chase her away. And he was aware he was precariously close to doing just that. Thinking she had never looked more beautiful than she did at that moment, with her hair falling in soft tousled waves to her chin and her fair skin glowing, Gabe said persuasively, "We haven't even given this a chance." One evening in bed was not reason enough to call it quits. Not when they could damn well try again. A lot more successfully this time.

But obviously, given the temper still burning hotly in her eyes, she didn't agree. "I'm still ovulating, Gabe," she informed him with brisk determination as she fixed him with a withering stare. "I plan to go to the fertility clinic this afternoon, pick a donor and get started. So you're off the hook. Now," she reached for her yellow legal pad and pen, "what do you want in terms of kitchen design?"

Gabe didn't give a damn what his kitchen looked like, but knowing this was the only way to get her to spend time with him, he contrived to make the rebuilding as difficult and complicated as possible. "First, it's got to be twice as big."

Maggie arched a warning brow, stated practically,

"That would really eat into the size of your great room."

"I don't care." Gabe turned his swivel chair to face her. Deciding to see how fast he could turn this work session from below zero to boiling, he let his glance rove slowly over her, taking in her slender legs, trim waist and generous breasts before returning his attention to her face. Aware she was already getting a little piqued with him, he smiled. "I want a kitchen that is large enough to cook in seriously. The one I had really wasn't."

"Then I recommend we go with either an L-shaped kitchen, or a U-shaped kitchen."

It was going to take some hard work on his part to get her to cool down where he was concerned. He didn't have much time, either if he was going to stop her from going back to the fertility clinic that afternoon and having a baby with someone—anyone—else.

"What's the difference?" Gabe asked as he struggled to keep his mind on the subject at hand.

Maggie reached for a sketch pad, and illustrated as she talked. "An L-shape has the appliances, cupboards and work stations or sinks arranged on two adjacent walls. The U-shape uses three."

Both options looked workable to Gabe. "Which do you prefer?"

Maggie didn't have to think about that. "If you

want your kitchen to have an unobstructed view of the beach—''

''I do,'' Gabe said firmly. He didn't cook a lot, but maybe that would change if he had someone he cared about to prepare meals with.

''Then the L-shape would be best,'' Maggie said emphatically. She drew a rectangular shape in the center of the L. ''I also suggest an island in the middle.'' She drew a square and four circles at one end. ''You can put your stove on that and it can be used for a breakfast bar as well.''

Gabe thought about that as he watched her soft, delicate-looking hands complete the sketch. ''Can I get an indoor grill?''

''Sure.'' Maggie drew in cupboards, and a place for a refrigerator and sink, too.

''Okay. Sounds good.'' Gabe stood. Now that the work was done, he was ready to play. And perhaps do a little courting and persuading as well. He took Maggie by the elbow. ''Let's go to lunch.''

Frowning, she resisted his chivalrous efforts to help her to her feet. ''We're not finished here, Gabe,'' she told him with a stern look. ''Besides, it's only 10:00 a.m. But if you want me to order in for you, I can do that.''

Gabe sighed, sat back down, and wished he couldn't recall quite so accurately how sweet that mouth of hers tasted or just how well she could kiss. ''No. I can wait.'' He wasn't hungry anyway. He just wanted her in a different setting, one more amenable to romance and persuasion. "So what else do we have to decide?" he asked casually.

"What kind of cabinets do you want?"

"I have no clue." Reluctantly, he tore his gaze from her trim figure, pushing the image of her in her pajamas out of his mind. He didn't need to recall how sexy she had looked, with only a single layer of peach silk sliding over her bare skin, when just the sight of her now, fully clothed, was enough to send the blood rushing to his groin. "What kind did I have before?" he asked curiously, not sure he had ever really looked.

But, of course, Maggie knew. "Cherry."

"To tell you the truth," Gabe said honestly, wanting her expert opinion on this, "they were a little dark."

Maggie didn't look surprised. "If you want your kitchen to be light, then I suggest white bead-board," Maggie said with a smile. "It has the timeless look of a country cottage."

"Sounds good," Gabe said enthusiastically. He completely trusted Maggie's taste. "But I want another ceramic tile floor."

Maggie nodded. Pulling her legal pad toward her again, she made additional notes. "Since you live at the beach, I agree that's a good choice, but this time I would put in a larger tile, laid on the diagonal, with small decorative tiles laid in between, and work it on into the living room."

She got up, went to the shelves behind her, and got out a heavy display board. Gabe liked the earth-toned sample she showed him. It was a mellow butterscotch color with deeper copper and ecru accents. He wasn't so sure however about continuing the tile into the adjoining space. "But the living room is carpeted," he reminded.

"It will give you a better flow between the two areas, once we knock out that dividing wall, to install tile in the entire area. Besides, if we expand the kitchen, part of that carpet is going to have to come up anyway." She touched his hand reassuringly. "Trust me. It'll look better this way and you can add a new rug in the conversation area in front of the fireplace to sort of soften the look and make it a little cozier in there."

What could Gabe say? He trusted her. "Okay."

Maggie smiled and got down another display board. "For countertops, your choices are laminate, solid surface, tile, granite or marble."

Gabe studied them all, deciding finally, "I like the look of black marble."

To his satisfaction, Maggie looked pleased with his decision. She made a note, and then went on to show him fixtures—he went with whatever she suggested. When it came to the appliances, he picked out all top of the line. Paint was next. She suggested a mossy green that meshed particularly well with the earth-toned floor and white cabinets. And a painted ce-

ramic-tile backsplash that brought all the colors together and worked well with the beaded cupboards
and the black marble.

"I think it's going to look great," he said.

"It will," Maggie promised confidently, as she tal-
lied up the price tag of his selections, printed out a
receipt and then showed it to him.

Gabe lifted his eyebrows in surprise. "Wow," he
said. Even for him this was steep.

"We can cut corners if you like, and bring the price
down." Maggie looked at him, waiting, perfectly
willing to do that if it was what he wanted.

Gabe shook his head, said firmly, "Nope. If we're
going to do this, we're going to do it right. I don't
want to do anything halfway."

Too late, Gabe realized what he had said. How it
could be construed. Especially in light of their recent
past.

Resentment flashed in Maggie's eyes, hot and
fierce, followed swiftly by hurt. "Too bad—" Maggie muttered beneath her breath as, avoiding his
stunned look, she rose with understated elegance to
show him out "—you didn't feel the same way last
night."

Chapter Six

"What did you say?" Gabe asked in a cool, deliberate tone as he followed her into the foyer.

Maggie turned to face him, making her expression as normal as she could make it, considering that he was glowering at her in a completely uncivilized manner. "Nothing."

"I think you did." His glance swept over her face before returning with slow deliberation to her eyes.

Maggie swallowed. Experience had taught her that emotional arguments left her feeling vulnerable, and she did not want to be vulnerable when she was with Gabe. The combination of the feelings in her heart and her dreams for the future had put her enough at risk already. She smiled at him as if she hadn't a care in the world. "I let my temper do the talking. I apologize."

His eyes steady, Gabe gave her a once-over that was anything but comforting. "Why should you apologize for saying what you feel?"

Maggie sighed and refused to notice how handsome he looked in his light blue polo shirt and casual stone slacks. She backed up until she felt the front door at her back. "Because telling you how I feel is only making things worse between us."

Gabe walked forward until he was standing right in front of her. He extended one hand, palm flat, and placed it on the wall next to her as he waited for her answer. "And how are things between us?"

Maggie wet her lips and, knowing it was imperative she keep a better grip on her spiraling emotions, willed herself to return Gabe's penetrating gaze with a tenacity that was, at the very least, equal to his. "How are things between us?" she echoed sarcastically. That was easy! "They're tense. Awkward. Awful."

Gabe released a beleaguered breath, dropped his hand, and stepped back slightly. He folded his arms in front of him, the action only serving more distinctly to outline the hard, masculine contours of his shoulders and chest beneath the soft knit fabric of his shirt. "It doesn't have to stay that way."

"You're telling me you can forget what we almost did last night? Our whole relationship has been a comedy of errors." Maggie stalked away from him. Finding herself suddenly unbearably thirsty, she walked into her kitchen and got a glass down from the cupboard. She filled it with water from the refrigerator and gulped thirstily.

"So we made a few mistakes."

"A few!" Maggie set her glass down on the counter with a thud. She ignored the way his dark, dangerous, oh-so-masculine presence was looming over her. "Try nothing but, Gabe!"

Gabe walked closer and picked up the glass she had set down. He drained the rest of the water from the glass, then fixed her with a way-too-patient glance that let her know she was in an even bigger fix than she had thought, because—inherent Good Samaritan that he was—he was about to come to her rescue once again. He put the glass aside, returned his gaze to her with a mixture of politeness and respect that almost undid her. "We can remedy this," he told her confidently.

How? Maggie wondered. By another good deed? Tears of frustration and sadness pooled in her eyes. She willed them not to fall, but they fell anyway. Maggie turned her back to him and felt her back graze the hardness of his chest. "Don't, Gabe," she said in a low, strangled voice.

He put his hands on her shoulders and turned her gently around to face him. His eyes softened as they searched her face. "Don't what?" he asked softly, abruptly looking as susceptible to the circumstances that were conspiring against them as she felt.

When he looked at her like that, when he touched her so tenderly and respectfully, it was all she could do not to fall head over heels in love with him. Hanging on to her composure by a thread, she shrugged free of his light, detaining grip, stepped past him. "Don't try to play the Good Samaritan with me again," she warned haughtily. "I know what you're trying to do here—"

He grinned, his attitude one of complete male confidence. "And what's that?" he asked patiently.

"Pursue me until I relent, and you finish the Good Samaritan task you started last night. The thing is," she warned in a low, fierce voice, "it's not necessary."

Gabe leaned closer in a drift of brisk, masculine cologne. He planted his hands on the counter on either side of her. The dark hue of his eyes, the firm, implacable set of his lips, gave him an even more rugged look than usual. "I beg to differ with you there, since you're my wife, you're ovulating, and you haven't changed your mind about getting pregnant."

Refusing to encourage his fantasies about making theirs a real marriage, in every sense, Maggie splayed her hands across the hardness of his chest and pushed. To her frustration, he didn't budge, not in the slightest. "The difference is, I no longer want you to father my child," she told him emotionally. "And I certainly don't want you making love to me!"

"Really?" he drawled.

Maggie drew herself up to her full height and glared at him warningly. She dropped her hands from the steely warmth of his chest, and folded them tightly in front of her, like a shield.

"Really!" she said, angling her chin up another notch.

Gabe merely smiled, wrapped both his arms around her anyway, and brought their bodies into full frontal contact. "Then let's put it to the test," he murmured as his lips traced a fiery, erotic path down the slope of her neck, behind her ear, across her jaw.

Hot tingles swept through Maggie. Her knees were so weak it was all she could do to stay on her feet. She glowered at him stubbornly, forcing herself to be as logical and cool as the situation demanded, when all she wanted was to be wild and passionate, completely swept away. "What are you talking about?" she demanded hoarsely, turning her head away.

Gabe caught her face between his hands and brought it right back to his. "Kiss me, and then tell me that."

Lips touching.

Refusing to give in to the pounding of her heart and the feeling inside her, she kept her lips firmly closed and herself stiff in his arms. "Convinced I mean what I say?" she taunted recklessly.

Gabe shook his head slowly, deliberately. "I'll only be convinced when you give me a real kiss and then tell me that," he said.

The dare in his eyes was impossible to resist. "All right," Maggie replied defiantly, knowing she was up for the challenge, for both their sakes she had to be. "If you insist." Her heart pounding, whole body trembling, Maggie thrust herself all the way into his arms, and opened her lips to the plundering sweeping motions of his tongue. And that was when everything predictable ended. He stole her breath, the passion in his deep, insistent kiss fueling her own. She tingled everywhere they touched, and everywhere they didn't. Despite herself, she began to respond as she felt his need and his yearning. Again and again they drew from each other, too swept up in the moment to let go. One instant Maggie was letting him take control, the next she was seizing the lead. Gabe shifted closer still, his tongue learning the sweet, damp contours of her mouth, touching her teeth, her lips, then returning in a series of long, tantalizing kisses that robbed her of the will and ability to think. "Damn you," she said on a shuddering breath, aware desire was flowing through her, more potent and mesmerizing than she had ever believed possible.

"Damn us both," Gabe agreed huskily, as he swept her into his arms and carried her down the hall and up the stairs to the master bedroom.

He helped her off with her blazer, her boots.

"This isn't going to mean anything," Maggie promised as she swiftly and methodically stripped off the rest of her clothes while he did the same, then climbed beneath the covers on her bed and brought them to her chin. She would never let him hurt—and desert—her again, the way he had the first time. "It's only a means to an end," she stated resolutely. To the baby they both wanted. Their baby.

Resplendent and unashamed in his nakedness, in much less of a hurry to get the necessary coupling over with, Gabe lifted the covers and climbed in after her. "Tell me that again later and I'll believe you," Gabe taunted with a sexy smile. He stretched out beside her and draped her body with the length of his. Immediately, she felt what she had only seen. Another hot rush of sensation swept through her, and then his lips were on hers once again and she tasted the hot, irrefutable force that was Gabe, felt his passion in the heat and danger of his kiss. She didn't want to surrender herself to him, she wanted to keep everything in the proper perspective, but his will was stronger than hers. With a low moan of surrender, Maggie tilted her head to give him better access. His lips meshed with hers, his manhood surged against her— hot, demanding—and Maggie knew this time there would be no going back. No chickening out for either of them.

"Now," Maggie murmured. *Before I lose my nerve.*

"Not," Gabe said, just as decisively, "until we're ready. We're not ready, Maggie. Either of us."

But Gabe was determined they soon would be. He rolled off her, peeled back the sheet, baring her to the waist. Maggie flushed all the hotter, behaving, he thought, like the virgin he knew she couldn't be. Nevertheless, he found her shyness appealing, and knew he had his work cut out for him if he was going to make her as at ease with him in the bedroom as he wanted her to be. ''You're beautiful,'' he murmured as he admired the softness of her fair skin. Her breasts were high and full, softly rounded globes with dusky rose centers, her waist slender.

Not content with just seeing her, he cupped the softness of her breasts in his hands, brushed his thumbs across her nipples, again and again until she moaned. Loving the way she trembled, even as her nipples budded, he bent his head and traced the rosy areola with his tongue, brushed it dry with his lips, then suckled her tenderly. Eager to know more of her, he kissed his way to her tummy, back again to her breasts, to the nape of her neck, then lower still. Past her waist, to the nest of curls hidden between her thighs. Trembling from head to toe at the long, sensual strokes of his lips and tongue, Maggie caught his head in her hands, tangled her fingers in his hair. She moaned again, ''Gabe,'' and this time it was an entreaty, a plea. Gabe paused and their eyes met. She looked so beautiful in her passion, so wanton with her cheeks flushed, her lips wet and open, that he felt himself responding wildly. He wanted to make her his, all the way, right now, and yet...he also wanted this night to be the fulfillment of every fantasy she'd ever had. He wanted to make sure she had exactly what she yearned for before they tended to his needs. So he parted her thighs all the wider and found her again, tracing the moist, tender petals, then plunging his tongue deep inside. Her head fell back, her body shuddered, and then she was throbbing all over, inside and out, falling apart in his hands. Satisfied at the way he was pleasing her, Gabe held her until the aftershocks had nearly passed, then moved swiftly upward. Wanting to prolong her pleasure the best way he knew how, he positioned himself and prepared to slip deep inside her.

And hit…resistance. Resistance he didn't expect.

Gabe paused, shocked, not sure whether to proceed or to ask the questions that obviously should have been asked before. And that was when Maggie took the lead. Her eyes fierce with yearning, her body melting against him in surrender, she opened her legs all the more, flattened hands on his hips, and brought him the rest of the way home, not stopping until he was surrounded by hot, silky warmth. Pleasure flooded through Gabe in fierce, unrelenting waves. The softness of her body giving new heat to his, he took her to the heights and depths. He showed her they didn't need to do anything but feel. He did everything he needed to do to make her his, not just for now, but for all time. Until Maggie arched against him, holding him just as close, kissing him just as deeply, until their mouths fused as intimately as their bodies.

Then need took over once again, making them both relentless. Reckless.

Lost in the swirling pleasure, Gabe lifted her hips and went deeper yet. Loving her fiercely until she clung to him, encouraging him with every kiss, every untutored stroke of her hands, and his blood ran hot and quick, Gabe once again took and kept the lead.

"This could be it, Maggie," he murmured wonderingly as he sought to make them one, not just in the physical sense, but in every respect—heart, mind, soul. "We could be making our baby right now." *The link that would meld—and keep—them together for all eternity.* And then all was lost, in the fierce ascent to oblivion, and the sweeter, softer fall back.

MAGGIE LAY ON HER BACK, eyes shut, catching her breath. She felt Gabe gently disengage their bodies and shift his weight off her. She had read enough about the mechanics of conception to know it was best that she stay right where she was, for the prescribed fifteen minutes after making love, to ensure the most favorable angle for the baby-making process.

"Why didn't you tell me?" he asked gently.

Unable to turn away, for fear of accidentally dislodging his seed, Maggie stared at the ceiling overhead. "Maybe because I thought it was obvious," she said, unable to help her flush.

Gabe's eyes widened. "That you were a virgin?"

Maggie wished she could run. Avoid all these questions. But she wanted a baby—Gabe's baby—too badly to risk negating what they had just done. She sighed, closed her eyes against his searching gaze, and did her best to hide a very acute case of embarrassment. "Why should it matter?" she asked him on a weary sigh. *Why did he care that she had been a failure in the lovemaking department for a very long time?*

"Because it does," Gabe said gently.

A very awkward silence fell between them. After a moment, Maggie slanted Gabe a glance. He had rolled onto his back too, and his forearm shaded his eyes, keeping whatever he was thinking or feeling from her view. "Why?" she whispered, even more insistently, needing to know.

Gabe rolled onto his side. He looked angry now—with himself. And with her—for not giving him a heads-up on the subject before they leapt into bed together. "Because you're my wife," he told her grimly, looking as if he felt as betrayed as she felt embarrassed. "And you've never made love with a man—until now. Even though you were engaged to be married."

Aha. There it was, she thought angrily, the sibling rivalry again.

"You want to know why Chase and I never made love," she guessed, wishing for the millionth time she had never been foolhardy enough to get engaged to Gabe's wildly successful older brother.

Gabe shrugged, his feelings suddenly more in check. "Chase is supposed to be the authority on women in the family," he pointed out with a tranquility Maggie guessed he couldn't really begin to feel. She sighed, knowing whether she liked it or not she absolutely had to explain the reasons behind the second biggest mistake in her life to Gabe. That was, if she wanted Gabe to understand her, and she did.

"There's no question Chase has the 'art of the chase' down pat," she said eventually.

Gabe's lips curved at her play on words. "So, if he is so good at pursuing a woman, then why didn't you let him make love to you?"

"Because he had such a reputation as a ladies' man and bachelor at large. I guess I was a little intimidated, given my lack of experience."

"Guys like their women to be innocent," Gabe said, eyeing Maggie with a depth of male speculation she found disturbing. He caressed the bare curve of her shoulder with a light, gentle touch. "It means a lot to be someone's first lover. To know that they waited for you."

Ignoring the way she tingled warmly at his slightest touch, Maggie tucked the top of the sheet around her breasts. She folded her arms in front of her matter-of-factly. She could feel the blood rushing to her cheeks, even as she struggled to get a handle on her soaring emotions. "You're reading a lot into this."

"There's a lot to read," he stated, his gaze raking

the length of her before returning to her face. He looked as though he had a lot more than just her virginity on his mind.

Maggie sighed. Feeling the flush on her face deepen warmly, she guessed, "You want to know why I made love to you and not him."

"Yes," Gabe said, as their knees collided beneath the sheet.

Maggie swallowed as she edged her knee away. "I told him I wanted to wait until we were married."

Gabe drew back slightly, to better study her face. "And Chase accepted that?"

"Yes." Almost too readily, Maggie thought in retrospect.

"But that wasn't really it," Gabe theorized.

How did Gabe see so much of what she was really thinking and feeling? "No," Maggie said.

"Then what was it?" Gabe persisted.

Maggie drew a deep, bolstering breath, afraid if she told Gabe everything she would look even more foolish and femininely inept in his eyes. "I was scared."

And ashamed of being so unenthusiastic about what was an integral part of every healthy marriage. At the time, she had blamed her earlier bad experiences in the bedroom for her anxiety. But now, she knew her resistance to the idea of going to bed with Chase had been rooted in something else.

"Of the man you were going to marry?" Gabe regarded her in cool disbelief.

Maggie bit her lip. "I wasn't frightened of Chase. I know there is nothing to be frightened about when it comes to Chase." Like Gabe, Chase was a gentleman to the core.

"Then...?" Gabe persisted, really wanting to understand.

Maggie shrugged and plucked at the sheet drawn over top of them. "Maybe it was just never right. Maybe I just never really wanted your brother to make love to me because I wasn't really in love with him, nor was he really in love with me."

Gabe frowned. "Then what was your engagement to him about?"

This, Maggie knew. "Because Chase pursued me the way I had always wanted to be pursued—with no holds barred," she explained. "And that fed my ego, big-time. The fact I wasn't initially interested in him at all only made him work all the harder, which he loved."

Gabe nodded, agreeing. "Because he's the kind of guy who loves a challenge."

"And I loved leading him on a merry chase," Maggie concluded with chagrin. "So in that sense our courtship was very exciting. And my life back then, when my parents were still alive and watching over me constantly, was about as far from exciting as one could get. I knew there was something not quite right between me and Chase all along, of course—"

Gabe's eyes gentled with understanding as he said

softly, "That something being that Chase was really in love with Bridgett Owens."

Maggie sighed her regret, thinking how much better hindsight was. "Right. But at the time, I just enjoyed the way he came after me. It was very flattering. And I mistook the thrill of our constant witty sparring for love. It was only after we got closer to the wedding day, and things were really set in stone, that the sparks between us began to fade, and I began to question if we really loved each other, or if it was all just a game."

"Which is where I came in," Gabe recalled, not quite happily.

Maggie nodded and continued plucking nervously at the sheet as she recalled that awful confusing time. "When I felt physically attracted to you, I knew I couldn't marry Chase. So I broke it off with him. But maybe that, too, was just a convenient excuse."

Gabe's brows knit together in confusion. "What do you mean?"

Maggie'd had a lot of time to think about and rationalize this—almost two years. She shrugged. "Maybe I wasn't really as attracted to you as I thought." Maybe even now she was fooling herself: incorrectly identifying her deepest emotions, such as they were, confusing physical desire with love. Because right now…here, with Gabe, in her bed, she was sure she had fallen in love with Gabe. Aware Gabe was waiting for her to continue, Maggie gulped.

"Maybe our chemistry wasn't as strong as I thought it was back then. Maybe I was just looking for an excuse to end my engagement and you were just handy."

"The way I'm handy now?" His low voice was self-assured and faintly baiting.

Maggie told herself the fifteen minutes were up. She started to get out of bed. "Yes."

His actions a lazy counterpoint to hers, Gabe reached over and brought her back down among the pillows once again. He smoothed the mussed hair from her face. "You can tell yourself that, if you want."

Maggie tried not to think how incredibly alive she felt whenever she was around Gabe. Never mind how much she had missed him during the two years they had avoided seeing each other as much as possible. "But you don't believe it," she guessed.

"No." Gabe regarded her steadily. "I don't."

"Now whose ego is involved?" Maggie demanded, her breath suddenly coming as erratically as the quickened pounding of her heart. The last thing they needed was to confuse their mutual desire to make a baby with anything remotely akin to love.

"It's not my ego you have to be worried about," he told her gravely, kissing her lips, her temple, her cheek. "It's my heart, Maggie. Because whether you want to admit it or not, we can't keep getting more and more involved with each other and keep our feelings out of it.''

But that was exactly what she had been trying to do! ''That's not what you said when you married me two days ago,'' Maggie reminded as he shifted over top of her.

''Two days ago,'' Gabe drawled, as he parted her knees and settled heavily between them once again, ''I didn't know we'd be doing this.''

Nor had she, Maggie thought, as Gabe bent his head, and with little protest from her after all, made hot, wild, passionate love to her again.

Chapter Seven

"Okay, you proved your point," Maggie conceded with a heartfelt sigh an hour later, as she rolled onto her stomach and buried her face in her pillow with a low anguished groan that didn't begin to reflect the depth of her conflict. She literally could not believe the way she and Gabe had just made love—not once, but twice. The heat of their passion had enveloped her in a pleasure unlike anything she had ever dreamed possible. It might have given her the baby she wanted so desperately. And yet at the same time, she knew she should have used a lot more common sense. In making love with each other they had not only crossed a line that probably never should have been crossed, they had simultaneously made their marriage legal and taken the informal prenuptial agreement they'd had and turned it upside down, adding intimacy and physical contact where there should have been none.

Gabe kissed his way across her shoulders, before

slipping his hands gently beneath her and turning her back over, so they were once again face-to-face. He looked down at her tenderly, making no effort at all to disguise how much he wanted and needed her, still. At least from a physical perspective. "And what point is that?" he asked as he smoothed a gentle hand down her body.

"That a physical attraction exists between us," Maggie confessed miserably, ignoring the tingling of her nipples and lower still, the butterflies of desire that began to build once again.

Before Gabe could reply, his beeper went off. Frowning, Gabe sat up and reached for his clothes, sorting through them until he found the electronic device. He silenced it and brought it back into bed with them, frowning as he read the flashing number on the screen. "It's the hospital."

Saved by the demands of his profession, Maggie thought. She slipped from the bed, grabbed her own clothes and headed for the bathroom.

By the time she shut the door, he was already on his cell phone. Maggie was grateful for the time to pull herself together. She didn't want to find herself making this lovemaking session out to be more than it was—a way to make the baby he had promised her without going to a clinic and using a cup and a syringe.

By the time she emerged from the bathroom, Gabe

was slipping on his slacks. The look on his face told her something troubling was going on.

"Jane Doe's suddenly taken a turn for the worse," he said, in answer to her unspoken question.

Maggie felt her heart go out to Gabe's patient. "I take it this means you still don't know who she is," she said, thinking how awful it must be for the elegant-looking older woman to be stuck in the hospital, all alone.

His expression both grim and perplexed, Gabe shook his head. "No, and it's the oddest situation. Aunt Winnifred and Harry went to see her. Jane Doe took one look at them, put the covers over her head and refused to talk to them."

Maggie watched as Gabe pulled his short-sleeved polo shirt on over his head. The knit fabric molded to his broad shoulders, muscled pecs and washboard abs. "You're kidding!"

"No." Gabe sighed as he tucked his shirt inside his slacks, and buckled his belt. "But then I guess it's no surprise," he admitted with the pragmatism of a physician who had seen and heard it all. "She's been acting—and talking—kind of kooky ever since she was admitted."

Maggie sat on the edge of the bed, while he put on his socks and shoes. "What about the television station?"

Gabe stood. Pulling a comb from his back pocket, he restored order to the wavy layers of his hair.

"They had some calls from people who were concerned, and a fund has been started for her at one of the local banks, and my aunt Winnifred has hired Harlan Decker, a private detective here in Charleston, to see if he can't help identify her, but thus far no one's been able to tell us who she is."

"That's awful," Maggie said. Seeing that Gabe was in a hurry to get going, she accompanied him down the stairs to the foyer.

"I guess that's what it's like when you don't have a family any longer," Gabe said.

Which was, Maggie thought as her sympathy for Jane Doe deepened, exactly why she wanted a child of her own so badly. She wanted to be connected with someone by blood again. She wanted that sense of family. In the meantime, though, maybe it was time she stopped feeling sorry for herself over her predicament and spent a little more time and energy helping others who were worse off than she. "Could I go to the hospital with you?" she asked impulsively. "To see Jane Doe?"

Gabe hesitated. She could see by the look on his face that he wanted her company. But he also wanted to protect her. "There's no guaranteeing she'll want to see you or anyone else," Gabe warned.

Maggie wasn't concerned about herself. "Please," she said softly, already grabbing her handbag and keys. "Maybe I can help her remember. She must have a home somewhere."

JANE DOE was propped up in bed, an oxygen tube going into her nose, when Gabe and Maggie walked into her room. Her wrinkled cheeks were flushed with fever, her eyes a little glazed, but she recognized Gabe immediately. "Why, Dr. Deveraux," she said, extending her hand as cordially as if they had just arrived for tea. "How nice of you to drop in to call on me."

"I'm happy to be here," Gabe said, smiling, as he gently took her hand and gave it a squeeze. Gabe put his stethoscope in his ears and listened to Jane Doe's heart and lungs, then checked the numbers on the electronic monitors next to her bed. Finished, he straightened again, asked, "So how are you feeling?"

"A little sad, actually."

"Any particular reason why?" Gabe asked, his dark brow furrowing.

Jane Doe moved her shoulders in a graceful shrug. "Does a broken heart count?" she asked, even more dispiritedly.

"Always," Gabe said gently. He pulled up a chair beside the bed, and asked, in a you-can-tell-me-anything-tone that was as familiar to Maggie as his kisses. "Did you recently lose someone you loved?" Gabe asked, even more kindly.

Jane Doe turned her head to the side, looked away. "I can't talk about that with you," she said as a single tear slipped down her cheek. "You're a man. You wouldn't understand."

Gabe looked at Maggie. She could tell he wanted her to try. She nodded imperceptibly, then moved around to the other side of the bed. She waited until Jane Doe looked at her. "I'm Maggie. I was here yesterday. Do you mind if I stay with you a while?" she asked considerately.

Jane Doe studied her warily. "Are you a social worker?"

Maggie smiled. "No. I'm just a friend of Gabe's."

"All right, then," Jane Doe said, looking visibly relieved.

"I'm going to go and see if I can't hurry the labs with the results of the tests that were taken just a while ago," Gabe said. He exited the room.

Maggie smiled at Jane Doe. "Can I get you some ice water?"

"Please."

"I hate for you to be here all alone," Maggie said sympathetically, as she poured some water from the plastic pitcher into a drinking cup.

The corners of her lips turning down in discouragement, Jane Doe looked down at the IV lines running into the backs of both her hands. "My time is running out. I can feel it."

Maggie put a straw in the cup and helped Jane Doe sit up enough to take a drink. "Oh, I think they can make you well."

"I hope so." The woman looked at Maggie earnestly. "I had so much left to do," she said emotionally. "I wanted everyone to be happy—as happy as I should have been."

Now, maybe they were getting somewhere, Maggie thought. "Who's everyone?" she asked casually. "Your family?"

Jane Doe smiled affectionately as she ran her hands restlessly over the snowy white thermal blanket on her bed. "My great-niece and nephews. Even my nephew and the woman he has always loved."

Glad to know she had a family somewhere, Maggie leaned forward earnestly. "If you tell me their names or where they live, maybe I can contact them for you." She so wanted this woman to have the happiness she so obviously deserved.

Jane Doe's eyes suddenly sparkled with devilish lights. She became as cagey as could be. "I'd rather talk about you," she said, suddenly looking and sounding stronger than she had since Maggie had arrived. "Is it my imagination? Or are you in love with that young doctor?"

GOOD QUESTION, Maggie thought. Prior to their afternoon of wild, uninhibited lovemaking, she would have said absolutely not, that although she was technically still his wife, she wasn't sure he was even a friend. Or ever would be.

Now...

Now, she didn't know.

She felt connected to Gabe.

More connected than she had to any man.

But whether that was simply because he was the first man—the only man—to ever make love to her, or if there was something more there—something special and unique and everlasting, she did not know.

"Because I have to tell you—I was watching him just now—and I think he might be in love with you," Jane Doe continued in a voice that was not to be denied.

As the conversation turned to her situation, Maggie felt a self-conscious flush move from her chest and neck into her face. "Gabe is your doctor."

"I know. That doesn't mean I'm not interested in him."

"Interested how?" Gabe said, coming back into the room, several plastic bags of liquid medicine in hand.

"I think you should be married and have a baby," Jane Doe said, making Maggie blush all the more.

"Actually," Gabe said, just as enthusiastically, looking directly at Maggie in a way that recalled their passionate lovemaking, the consummation of their marriage and the possibility that they had made a baby that very afternoon, "so do I."

He hung the bags on the hooks at the top of the IV pole. "I thought nurses were supposed to do that," Maggie said, attempting to change the subject.

Gabe gave her a knowing look but answered her question anyway. "Usually they do, but the nurses are busy, and I wanted to get this started right away, so I'm going to do it.''

"What kind of medicine are you giving me?" Jane Doe asked curiously.

"These are both antibiotics to fight the pneumonia you've developed," Gabe said, his concentration on the complicated task at hand.

"I thought you were already giving me an antibiotic for that," Jane said.

Gabe slanted her a brief, reassuring glance as he switched her medicines around. "I'm going to try two different ones. I think they'll work a little better."

"What other medications am I getting?" Jane Doe asked, beginning to look as if she had completely depleted what little energy she had.

"IV fluids, an anti-inflammatory medicine to help bring down the swelling and speed the healing in your sprained ankle, and medications for pain or to help you sleep, as you need them," Gabe explained.

"Speaking of sleep." Jane Doe closed her eyes. "I'd like to take a nap, now. But you come back and see me, Maggie," she said, yawning. "You, too, Dr. Deveraux."

"WERE YOU ABLE to find out anything?" Gabe asked as soon as he and Maggie walked back out into the hall.

"Unfortunately, no." Maggie conceded with a disappointed sigh as she led Gabe to a deserted window at the other end of the hall, where they could talk privately. She settled into the corner and tilted her head up at him. "But she doesn't really seem all that confused today. I think she knows more about who she is than she is letting on—she's just not telling us everything."

Gabe lounged against the wall, and tucked his thumbs in the belt loops on either side of his fly. He studied her seriously. "What do you mean?"

In a low, hushed voice, Maggie quickly brought him up to speed. "Well, she talked about not having much time left, and wanting to see her extended family—a nephew and the woman he loved, and some great nephews and a niece—happy."

Gabe's brow furrowed. He leaned closer yet. "Did she mention any names?"

"No. But that—along with her 'broken heart'— made me wonder. Do you think it's possible her family recently put her in a nursing home."

"I'd think the nursing home would have reported her missing."

He had a point, Maggie thought. She pursed her lips together thoughtfully. "Well, what if the family was about to do that, and Jane Doe didn't want to go? So she ran away, and ended up here in Charleston. She could have just been seeing the sights in the historic district, or taking her daily constitutional when she fell. It's a lovely place, and very safe, even late at night. A lot of the downtown hotels are within walking distance of Gathering Street, for someone who's in decent physical shape. And it looks as if prior to her fall, Jane Doe was.''

Gabe ran a hand beneath his jaw, his fingers caressing the beginnings of five o'clock stubble that made him look even more ruggedly handsome than usual. ''I hadn't thought about that,'' he said, his eyes darkening.

Maggie's theory picked up speed. ''Maybe Jane Doe's afraid if she goes back to her family or lets them know what has happened, her family will use her fall and/or declining health and advancing age to force her into a retirement home, whether she wants to go or not.''

Gabe compressed his lips, and regarded Maggie thoughtfully. ''Do you think we should start a statewide search?''

Maggie shook her head—the last thing she wanted to do was hurt that nice woman. ''I think we should let Jane get well before we pressure her any more about her identity. Maybe in the meantime, she'll get to know us a little better and trust us enough to confide in us.''

''All right,'' Gabe said quietly. ''I'll tell the news stations to call off the dogs, so to speak, for a few days.''

''Thank you.'' Maggie breathed a sigh of relief. She didn't know how or why she had become Jane Doe's chief advocate. Maggie only knew in some way she couldn't explain that her happiness, and Gabe's, were intricately connected with Jane's.

"But in the meantime, you've got to try and keep making a connection with her," Gabe continued in a stern tone as he and Maggie walked back down the hall, toward the elevators. "Because if we don't know who she is when she is ready to be released from the hospital, Jane Doe probably will end up in a nursing home, and one not of her choosing, at that."

GABE AND MAGGIE were heading out of the hospital when they ran into Penny Stringfield in the parking lot. The pretty nurse had a manila envelope with her name on it clutched to her chest and it was clear she had been crying. "Uh-oh," Gabe said.

"Maybe you should go talk to her," Maggie suggested.

"Not without you," Gabe said firmly, taking Maggie's hand.

Before Maggie could do more than utter a protest, they were standing next to Penny who was attempting—unsuccessfully, it seemed—to unlock the door to her car. "What's going on?" Gabe asked in the low tone of a caring friend and co-worker.

Penny ducked her head, her eyes full of shame. "I can't talk about this with Maggie here," she sniffed.

"Sure you can," Gabe said, encouraging her. When Penny said nothing, he touched her shoulder and forced her to look at him. "Listen to me, Penny.

You can trust Maggie, the same way you can trust me. And we both want to help you.''

Her hands shaking so badly she could hardly hold on to her keys or the envelope, Penny looked at Maggie for confirmation.

Maggie promised quietly but firmly, ''Whatever you say to us will be held in strictest confidence.''

''Okay, but not here.'' Penny sobbed all the harder. ''We'll have to go to my motel room. I can't chance anyone overhearing us.''

Gabe declared Penny not fit to drive, and ushered both women into his car. Maggie sat in the front. Penny slumped in the back, not speaking, still crying. Fifteen minutes later, they were in a small motel room in the suburbs. Maggie and Gabe sat down in the two straight-backed chairs on either side of the small round table next to the window, and Penny sank down on one of the double beds. She handed Gabe and Maggie the envelope. ''This came for me at work today.''

Inside were black-and-white photographs of Penny and a man, kissing and embracing. Maggie knew they hadn't been taken recently—Penny's hair was past her shoulders now, in the photos she was wearing it in a short style that barely touched her ears.

Gabe looked up, amazed. ''You're being *black-mailed?*''

Penny nodded, and cried all the harder. ''I nearly had an affair the second year I was married to Lane.

Fortunately, I came to my senses after just one clandestine meeting and a few kisses. I told Walker it was a mistake, and refused to see him again. I thought that was the end of it until a few weeks ago, when I started getting these phone calls.''

Gabe's jaw tightened with displeasure. "From Walker?"

"Yes." Penny rubbed her red, swollen eyes. "He said he had never gotten over the way I had dumped him, and he was going to make me pay.''

What a nightmare, Maggie thought, her heart going out to Penny.

"Did you give him money?" Gabe demanded.

Penny took another deep, hiccuping breath. "Five hundred dollars. Twice. That was all I had in my savings.''

"But he wanted more," Maggie guessed, rummaging in her purse until she found some tissues. She handed them to Penny, who accepted them gratefully.

"Yes." Penny wiped the tears from her face and blew her nose. "And that's why I left Lane. I didn't want him to be hurt by any of this, and I knew he would be—terribly—if he found out, so I moved out. I hoped that if my marriage was already 'over' Walker would realize it wouldn't do any good to blackmail me any more, and move on.''

"Only he hasn't moved on," Gabe guessed.

"Merely upped the stakes," Maggie added.

Penny nodded, looking even more devastated. "I just don't know what I'm going to do."

"That's easy. You have to tell Lane the truth," Gabe said sternly.

"But then he'll know that I almost had an affair," Penny cried.

"He'll also know that you were set up from the get-go," Maggie said practically, pointing to the photos. "Otherwise, Walker wouldn't have any evidence to blackmail you with now."

Gabe concurred with Maggie. "Lane'll be hurt. He may even be angry. But I also know he loves you, Penny, and wants to know the reason you've been acting the way you have," Gabe continued firmly.

"But what if he never forgives me?" Penny asked, starting to cry all over again.

"Then at least he'll know the truth," Gabe said, looking upset for reasons, Maggie thought, that had very little to do with Penny, and everything to do with him. "And you'll know you did the right thing in the end."

Chapter Eight

"That really bothered you, didn't it?" Maggie said, as she and Gabe walked out to the motel parking lot. Directly behind Gabe's sports car was a big tour bus, blocking their exit from the lot. Groups of slow-moving sightseers were disembarking from the bus, bags and parcels in hand. It was barely time for dinner, and yet they all looked absolutely exhausted.

"What?" Gabe looked across the street, where mobile souvenir and snow-cone stands had been set up, and were now doing brisk business.

Maggie cast a brief, longing look at the icy treats being distributed, before turning back to Gabe. "The fact that Penny didn't tell her husband what was going on."

"Yes, it did." Gabe took her elbow and ushered her across the street, where they stood in line and ordered two large snow cones. Cherry for her, grape for him.

"Any particular reason why?" Maggie continued

her quest to understand him as the two of them strolled a little farther down the street, until they reached a cluster of shops, with a central outdoor atrium.

"Probably because I identify with Lane." Gabe said shortly, as he led her over to a park bench beneath a shade tree.

Maggie tilted her head to the side and drew another, deeper breath. "Because—?"

Gabe frowned as he sat down beside her. Lips compressed grimly, he said, "Because I was in a similar situation once. Involved with a woman who decided not to tell me the truth about what was really going on with her."

Maggie could see his hurt behind the matter-of-fact words. "It sounds serious."

"It was." Silence fell between them as they both sipped on their snow cones.

"I'd really like to hear about it," Maggie encouraged finally.

Gabe blew out an uneasy breath, looking less willing than ever to confide in her. But to his credit he turned his eyes to her and continued anyway, in a low, gruff tone, "It happened when I was eighteen. I was still reeling from my parents' divorce and all the turmoil in the family, and I got a lot more involved with my high-school girlfriend than I should have."

Maggie could tell by the anguished look on his face

the worst was yet to come. "Involved in what way?" she asked warily.

"Sexually—we were sleeping together and we were way too young."

Maggie blinked, amazed. That didn't sound like the Gabe she knew. He was Mr. Responsibility, always putting others' needs above his own. She could tell by the guilt in his eyes that he wasn't proud of what he had done. "Did she cheat on you—the way Penny nearly cheated on Lane?" Maggie asked curiously, still struggling to make the connection.

Gabe shook his head, at peace about that much. After a moment, he continued in a voice that was low, sad, introspective. "Just the opposite. Lynnette was really devoted to me, and I was to her. But we were still pretty young and we both knew it. Anyway, when we were about to head off to college—I was going to Duke in North Carolina and she was going to the University of Pennsylvania, Lynette asked me to elope with her." Gabe shook his head. Finished with his snow cone, he got up and threw the wrapper away. Maggie did the same.

The two of them sat back down on the bench, and Gabe stretched his long legs out in front of him and shoved his hands in the pockets of his slacks. "I thought she was nuts. I mean I loved her—but marriage? At eighteen? When we weren't even going to be living in the same state?"

"So you said no."

Gabe nodded grimly. He looked even sadder and more regretful as he said, ''What Lynnette hadn't told me was that she was pregnant with my baby or that soon after arriving in Philadelphia, she'd had a miscarriage. I don't know why Lynnette didn't go to a doctor, or get the medical attention she needed. Maybe she was afraid or thought if she ignored the symptoms they would just go away. In any case, her roommate thought Lynnette just had the flu. By the time they got her to the emergency room, it was too late. The resulting pelvic infection was so massive, she died a few hours later. Her parents blamed me, and I blamed myself, too,'' Gabe confessed, looking angry and upset with himself once again. ''I had obviously let Lynnette down in some fundamental way, even before she asked me to elope with her. Otherwise, she would have just told me she was pregnant. And I would have married her and been the best husband and father in the world to her and the baby. But she didn't give me the chance to make things right. Lynnette just assumed—the way Penny Stringfield is assuming now—that I wouldn't do the right thing or stand by her.''

''Oh, Gabe,'' Maggie said softly, her heart going out to him. ''I'm so sorry about your loss.'' She could see it had hurt him terribly. Wanting desperately to comfort him, the way he had comforted her when she was hurt, she reached over and touched his arm. ''Is that when you decided to break all records being a

Good Samaritan?'' No one did more good deeds than Gabe. And his efforts made sense to her now in a way they hadn't before—Gabe was still trying to make up for what had happened then.

Gabe nodded. He took his hands out of his pockets, covered both her hands with both of his, and looked deep into her eyes. ''I promised myself I would never be responsible for anyone's unhappiness again. That's why I wasn't able to be with you, after you ended your plans to marry my brother, even though we both knew how attracted we were to each other. I didn't want to hurt Chase or the rest of the family. But now that Chase has found his own happiness and given us his blessing to pursue whatever this is between us, I know it's all right.''

Maggie felt free to be with Gabe, too, though she hadn't really ever felt she needed Chase's permission. She just wasn't sure that Gabe was pursuing her for the right reasons. Was marrying and impregnating her just another act of kindness on his part—an effort to keep righting his wrongs? she wondered uneasily, as they stood and headed back to the parking lot where he'd left his sports car. Or, even more disturbing yet, was it an unconscious attempt to—in some way— replace the woman and baby he had lost so many years ago?

Maggie wished she could say it wasn't an attempt at soul-deep redemption.

But knowing Gabe, knowing how good and decent

and kind he was at heart, knowing how guilty and upset he still felt, she couldn't quite say the two things weren't connected in his heart and his soul.

MAGGIE COULD TELL Gabe was concerned about the determined way she kept the conversation on the rebuilding of his kitchen during the drive back to her place. So she wasn't surprised when he parked the car in her driveway and took her hand in his. Looking at her as if there were only one reply she could possibly make, he suggested softly, "Have dinner with me."

Maggie's heart skipped a beat at the ardor she saw reflected in his eyes. "Just dinner?" she asked lightly.

Gabe shrugged and looked at her with complete honesty. "I've got to admit," he said in a low, persuasive voice, "I wouldn't mind making love with you again."

Maggie knew if she made love with him again— that night—she wouldn't just fall in love with him, she would begin to feel as if they were really married to each other. As much as she secretly wanted that to be the case, she knew it really wasn't. "We set this up as a business arrangement, Gabe," she reminded persistently.

Gabe shrugged and tightened his grip on her hands. "Family business, maybe," he conceded.

Was Gabe her family? Maggie wondered. Or, assuming that they had made a baby that very afternoon, just her child's? Confused, her head spinning with her need for him, Maggie wedged distance between them, and said, "I need time to think about everything that's happened. I think you do, too."

Gabe didn't deny that was the case as they both got out of the car. He merely strolled around to her side of the car and said, "If you're still ovulating— if you haven't gotten pregnant yet—I think we should keep trying."

Maggie did, too. But not when she was still feeling so vulnerable and mixed-up.

She swallowed hard around the tension in her throat. "Tomorrow will be soon enough," she said firmly.

Gabe looked at her as if he wanted to make love to her all night long. "If you change your mind, all you have to do is call me."

MAGGIE *DID* CHANGE her mind, about a thousand times. But, determined not to confuse Gabe's hot and heavy pursuit of her for something more permanent and lasting the way she had before with Gabe and with his brother Chase, she stopped herself from calling Gabe. Instead, she concentrated on making sure she had all the materials needed for his kitchen ordered, via fax, by the end of the evening. Then she took a long bubble bath and fell into bed, exhausted, to dream all night long of Gabe and the way he had made love to her that afternoon.

Morning found her at Gabe's place, still wanting

him and wondering at the wisdom of her actions—potential baby or no. But there was no sign of Gabe. When he finally did arrive—in the same clothes he had been wearing when he dropped her off at her place the night before—it was clear, from his unshaven face and red-rimmed eyes, that he had been out all night.

"Rough night?" Enrico asked, giving Gabe the speculative once-over.

Maggie knew what Enrico was thinking—he was thinking Gabe had been out painting the town red with some other woman.

"And then some," Gabe confirmed, yawning. "We had several critical patients admitted at the hospital last night." He dragged a weary hand over his face. "All I want to do is fall into bed."

"Uh—only one problem with that," Maggie said.

"We're going to be hammering," Luis explained.

"And drilling and sawing," Manuel added.

Gabe looked pained. And, if possible, even more desperately in need of rest.

Maggie knew there was only one thing to do. "You can sleep at my place," she said. All eyes turned upon her. The room vibrated with the weight of the male disapproval turned her way.

"I think it's up to the client to find his own sleeping arrangements," Enrico cut in not so delicately.

"Yes," Luis agreed, in the same tone, as he glared

at Gabe. "That isn't something the business normally provides."

"I also think Dr. Deveraux should sleep at a friend or family member's place," Manuel weighed in, sending a paternal look Maggie's way.

Maggie had no doubt her parents would have said the same, had they been here to see her make such an unusual offer. Unfortunately for her three crew members, Maggie wouldn't have been prone to take her folks' advice on the subject either.

"Listen, guys," Maggie said, pleasantly, as she fished the keys out of her pocket. She shot Manuel, Luis and Enrico firm looks. " I know you mean well, but I can make these decisions all by myself."

Gabe waved off her offer. "It's no problem. I can go to a hotel," he said.

"Actually, it is a problem." Already removing the house key from her key ring, Maggie turned back to her crew decisively. If she let them get away with telling her how to live her life once, they would think it was their male duty to keep doing it. And that she did not want, no matter how well-meant the interference. "I'm a grown woman," she reiterated patiently, her low precise tone of voice clearly emphasizing every word. "I know what I'm doing."

Luis, Manuel and Enrico gave her mutually skeptical looks.

"And I say Gabe sleeps at my place today," Maggie continued firmly, handing Gabe the key. "Now let's take a look at those plans, shall we?'' She shoved the key ring back into her jeans pocket and headed out to the kitchen, her work boots ringing authoritatively with every step she took.

GABE KNEW it was a bad decision on Maggie's part—even before he saw the looks from her trio of protectors. Nevertheless, he felt duty-bound, as a friend, lover and a secret husband, to support her in whatever choice she made. Especially when it came to her construction business and private life. He owed her that and, given the fact that she had brought love and joy back into his life, not to mention the possibility of a baby he had wanted for a very long time but didn't feel he deserved, so much more.

As he could have predicted, however, her crew was not about to let the situation pass unremarked. While Maggie disappeared briskly, Manuel, Enrico and Luis lagged behind. Muscles flexed, legs braced as if for battle, they surrounded Gabe, like a very quiet, very determined mob. ''Maggie may be our boss, but we watched her grow up and we love her like our own kids,'' Manuel hissed.

''I understand,'' Gabe said, just as seriously, but in a low voice. He didn't want Maggie hearing any of this, either.

''You are not to hurt her,'' Luis warned Gabe with a threatening scowl, looking quite willing to pummel sense into him if necessary, "or further damage her reputation in any way."

"Because if you do," Enrico promised, as gravely as Maggie's own father would have, had he still been alive, "you will be dealing with us."

"And we promise you," Manuel finished heavily, reminding Gabe of the way he had hurt not just Maggie—but others in the past—"this time it won't matter what Maggie says. We won't let you get away with it."

LUIS, ENRICO AND MANUEL'S thinly veiled threat still ringing in his ears, Gabe headed over to Maggie's beach house. Only after he had let himself in and headed for the bedroom did he realize he had forgotten to bring any clean clothes with him. Too tired to drive back to his own place, and for certain too guilty to subject himself to another well-deserved but withering lecture from Maggie's trio of protectors, Gabe headed for her shower. Feeling weary to the bone, he washed off the grime from the last twenty-four hours, toweled off, and then headed—buck naked—for her bed. He figured, as he climbed between the scented sheets of her bed, that his lack of clothing wouldn't matter. He'd be up and out of there long before she returned.

Gabe's head hit the pillow. Seconds later, he was asleep.

He woke around 4:00 p.m. Aware he'd done nothing but dream of Maggie the entire time he'd been in her bed, he rubbed the sleep out of his eyes and sat up. And that was when he heard a woman's high-pitched exclamation of dismay and the crash of something heavy hitting the covered porch below.

Gabe threw back the covers and raced to the bay windows overlooking the open-air porch. He looked down, expecting to see Maggie. Instead, there was a young woman who couldn't have been more than twenty years old, with a freckled face and waist-length curly red hair. She was wearing a bathing suit, nylon shorts and running shoes, and she had knocked a heavy clay planter full of geraniums off a patio table. It lay shattered at her feet. Backing up, an expression of mingled panic and dismay on her face, she dropped a note onto the painted wooden floor next to the sliding glass doors, covered it with a broken piece of pottery, and then headed back down the stairs leading up to the porch.

"Hey!" Gabe said, but she was already running full-speed down the beach.

Wondering what had the young girl so panicked—if she knew Maggie at all, she had to know Maggie would not be angry about a busted planter that could easily be replaced—Gabe walked back into the bathroom to splash some cold water on his face. Straightening, he grabbed a hand towel and blotted his face. And that was when he heard the soft feminine gasp of dismay. He pulled the towel away from his face,

and saw Maggie standing in the middle of her bedroom. She was still in her work clothes: nice-fitting
jeans, a long-sleeved navy-blue T-shirt and work
boots, and she was blushing fiercely as her gaze
dropped, almost unavoidably, to his crotch.

Figuring it was too late to be upset about her seeing
him sans clothes, and knowing there was little he
could do about his instantly aroused state anyway,
Gabe reached for his boxer shorts and slipped them
on over the part of his anatomy that was already hard
as a rock.

"Did you see that girl?" Maggie demanded, re-
covering her composure at long last.

Loving the pink blush of awareness in her cheeks,
the innocence in her green eyes, Gabe smiled. "The
one who broke your planter? Yeah, I did."

"Who is she?" Maggie demanded, putting her
hands on her slender hips.

Was it his imagination, Gabe wondered, or were
her nipples suddenly pearling beneath the soft clinging knit of her T-shirt?

Gabe shrugged and tried not to think about how
nice it would be if he could get Maggie nearly naked,
too. He was sure if they made love again, she'd begin
to trust him a little more, as there were things that
touch and a decided lack of inhibitions could convey
a lot better than words any day. Not that she seemed
to be wishing for the same thing—no, she looked as
if she wanted to erect an electric fence around her.

Anything to protect her heart and the successful solo life she had built for herself.

Aware Maggie was waiting—rather impatiently, it seemed—for him to answer her question, and that his lower half was throbbing, Gabe shrugged his broad shoulders and said, ''I have no idea who the girl was. I've never seen her before in my life.''

''Well, she left this.'' Maggie handed him the note. It was written on fine quality ivory stationery and stained with potting soil.

Their hands brushed as Gabe accepted it. His fingers tingling from the brief but potent contact, he opened the note up and read the scrawled words out loud, ''Jane Doe has a family. They just don't know it.''

Frowning, he turned the note over to see if anything else had been written on it, but it was blank. He looked back at Maggie. ''What does that mean?'' he demanded.

Maggie spread her hands wide, exclaimed, ''Heck if I know.'' She stared at Gabe, perplexed, ''Why would that girl tell me, anyway?''

Gabe took a moment to consider. ''Maybe she knows you've visited Jane Doe at the hospital,'' he speculated, at last.

''How would the girl know that?'' Maggie asked, as Gabe put on his slacks.

''Maybe Jane Doe told her—she's got a phone next to her bed. She can call out whenever she wants,''

Gabe suggested, sniffing his shirt. Unfortunately the clothes he had worn the day before smelled and felt like it.

"Would the hospital have a record of those calls?" Maggie asked, pacing around and giving him wide berth.

"No," Gabe replied decisively. Wishing for a razor and a toothbrush and the time he needed to make himself as presentable as he needed to be to woo Maggie the way she deserved to be wooed, Gabe sat down and put on his shoes and socks. "You might be able to get the information from the phone company, but it would take a court order to get it."

"And that would take time," Maggie pointed out unhappily, relaxing slightly as she perched on the bench in front of her dressing table.

"Time we don't really have," Gabe agreed. Like Maggie, he was worried about what was going to happen to Jane Doe if they couldn't earn her trust, and soon.

Maggie bit into her soft lower lip uncertainly. "Should we hand this note over to the police?"

Trying not to think how much he wanted to kiss her, Gabe shook his head. "I'll call Harlan Decker— the private detective my aunt Winnifred hired—and tell him about it. But then I think we should go to the hospital," he told Maggie firmly. "Talk to Jane Doe, show her the note, and see what she has to say about it."

Hope suddenly sparkled in Maggie's eyes. "You think if we show her the note that we might have a shot at getting Jane Doe to remember who she is?"

Gabe shrugged, not about to make any promises on what would or would not happen with his elderly patient. "It's worth a try."

Maggie straightened and cast a disparaging look at the dirt smeared on the thighs of her jeans. "I need to change clothes before we go," Maggie said.

"So do I," Gabe said, relieved he was finally going to get the opportunity to get their evening started off on a better note.

"How about I meet you at your place in twenty minutes?" Maggie said.

Gabe nodded. No doubt about it. Their evening was definitely looking up. "See you then."

MAGGIE TOLD HERSELF she was showering and putting the pretty sage-green sheath and matching short-sleeved linen jacket on for her visit with Jane Doe. The same went with doing her hair in a quick upsweep and putting on a pair of gold earrings. Her efforts to make herself look as nice as possible had absolutely nothing to do with the look of distinctly male appreciation she saw in Gabe's eyes the second he laid eyes on her.

"You look very pretty," Gabe said, as he let her in. He smiled at her sexily. "Smell good, too." He stopped just short of her and looked at her as if he very much wanted to kiss her again. "New perfume?"

Finding his low husky voice a bit too determined, too full of erotic promise for comfort, Maggie turned away with a cheerful grace she couldn't begin to really feel. "Same old one."

"Hmm." He followed her into the hall.

Maggie turned back to face him. Needing something concrete to focus on—besides the ever-mounting physical and emotional attraction between them— she nodded at his disheveled state. Although she had gone all out getting ready for their—well, it wasn't exactly a date, more like a casual, meaningless evening out—he still hadn't shaved. His mouth smelled minty fresh-like toothpaste and wintergreen mouthwash. He had on a clean pair of stone-colored khakis. But he was bare-chested and barefoot. And the damp, mussed state of his inky black hair indicated that— just like her—he had taken a shower too.

Trying hard not to think how alluring and faintly dark and dangerous the stubble of a day's worth of beard made him look, Maggie swallowed and plastered her most devil-may-care expression on her face. "I thought you were going to be ready to go," she said casually.

Gabe nodded his regret. "I was, but the hospital called me practically the moment I got out of the shower—they needed to bring me up to date on one of my patients. I just got off the phone a second ago.

In the meantime, I need to iron a shirt, and shave before I go.'' He strode toward the stairs, then paused and turned his gaze in the direction of the construction area. He looked at her with gratitude and respect. ''By the way, the kitchen is looking great.''

Maggie couldn't help it—she beamed with pleasure. ''You like what we've done so far?'' She couldn't say why, she just knew she wanted his approval.

Gabe nodded. ''Very much.''

Maggie turned her gaze in the direction of his and tried to see the ongoing project through her client's eyes. The walls had been taken out, the new framing was in place. Deciding as long as they were both here, they might as well go over the changes made thus far, Maggie took Gabe's hand in hers and led him into the center of the construction. She let go of his hand and continued, explaining proudly, ''As you can see, the electrical work has all been done, and the kitchen re-plumbed. You'll be able to put in the refrigerator that you wanted, with an icemaker and water in the door.''

Gabe leaned in closer to her ear. ''Where is the trash compactor going to go?''

Her heart pounding, Maggie leaned back slightly. She was tingling all over. She told herself it was excitement about her work causing her body to go haywire and not his proximity. ''Right here.'' Feeling the blood rush to the center of her body, Maggie stepped away from Gabe with as much grace as she could muster and pointed to an area of framed cupboard next to the new kitchen sink. "We're also going to build in recycling bins next to that."

"Great." Gabe looked impressed. He moved to join her, bracing a hand on the counter, just to the left of her. "When is the new flooring going in?"

Nerves jangling, Maggie danced away from him. "As soon as we get the cabinets in—so they'll probably start that tomorrow," she said with an efficient smile.

Gabe straightened and crossed his arms against the satiny smooth skin of his rock-solid chest. "It's really going to look great."

"I think so, too." Maggie tried not to think of how much she was going to miss not having an excuse to see him multiple times every single day. "You did an excellent job of picking out everything," she continued pleasantly.

"The problem is," Gabe said as he continued to survey their surroundings, the corners of his sensual lips turning down, "the rest of the house is going to look less than spectacular in comparison."

He had a point there, Maggie thought. The rest of his beach house was sorely in need of additional work. "So continue with the renovations, as you can," Maggie suggested. That's what she had done with her own place.

Gabe turned back to her with a smile. He looked

as if he had been hoping she would say that. "Will you help me?"

Maggie's pulse kicked up another notch. What was he really suggesting here? "Help you what?" she asked warily.

He shrugged his broad shoulders and locked eyes with her deliberately. "Decide what to do with my bedroom."

Chapter Nine

"You can be honest," Gabe said several minutes later as he plucked a pair of clean socks from a dresser. "I need help, don't I?"

Maggie watched as Gabe unfolded the pressing board attached to the back of his closet door, and plugged in an iron. "I'm the wrong person to ask," Maggie replied as he disappeared into the half-empty walk-in closet, and emerged with a blue dress shirt and a can of spray starch. "I always look at a room and see a million ways it could be improved."

Gabe shrugged and sprayed his shirt liberally. "So tell me how to improve this," he said.

Trying not to notice how sexy Gabe looked in just his stone-colored slacks, Maggie backed up until her hips touched one of two large dressers with attached mirrors. She folded her arms in front of her. "Bedrooms really aren't my forte."

"So help me anyway." Gabe's eyes shimmered

with a sexy, appealing light. "If it were your bed-room, how would you improve it?"

Happy to focus on anything that would keep her mind off the direction it really wanted to go—which was how much fun it would be to make love to Gabe again. Here. Now— Maggie turned her attention to the dècor. Or lack thereof. Her natural nesting in-stincts coming into play, she surveyed the dark, un-appealing master bedroom. It was masculine, all right. Too masculine. "Well, I'd take those heavy paisley drapes off the windows and replace them with white wooden blinds that could be opened or shut at will."

Gabe nodded agreeably as he pressed the wrinkles out of the collar. "What else?"

Maggie studied the spacious room. "I'd paint the room a soothing pale blue and customize the closet with drawers and shelving that would hold all your clothing. Then I'd take out both of these dressers."

Gabe quirked his brow in surprise.

Maggie smiled and explained, "You wouldn't need them anymore and they take up a lot of floor space." She moved away from the bureau. "I'd hide the TV and stereo equipment in a nice walnut armoire that matches your bed and place it here." Maggie pointed to that space on the wall. "And add a cozy reading chair in the corner by the window and a low book-shelf that doubles as a window seat there."

Gabe grinned at her enthusiasm. "Wow." Finished with the sleeves, he turned to the back of the shirt.

Warming to her subject, Maggie strolled closer to his king-size bed. "I'd also add some sort of print comforter and lots of extra pillows on your bed, and I'd cut a door into this wall here." She walked back to demonstrate. "And connect this bedroom to the small room next door so it could function as either a study or a nursery, depending on a person's needs." She turned back to Gabe excitedly. Able to clearly envision everything she had described, she explained the rationale behind her proposed improvement. "You'd still have a spare bedroom and a hall bath, which would make the place as easy to sell as ever. You never want to make improvements that would turn off potential buyers, or make a place unmarketable in the future. Because you never know when you're going to have to sell."

Gabe turned off his iron and bent to unplug it from the wall. "So when can you start?" Gabe asked.

Maggie blinked. "What?"

Gabe slid his arms into the sleeves of his shirt. "Doing all that for me, too."

Maggie tried to keep a handle on her runaway pulse. "We weren't talking about what *you* wanted here, Gabe," she reminded as he closed the distance between them, and lazily began buttoning up his shirt. "We were talking about what *I* wanted."

Half of Gabe's mouth turned up in a sensual smile. "I know."

Maggie gulped as he fastened the buttons on his sleeves. "So...?"

"So," Gabe undid his fly and tucked the tails of the shirt inside the waist of his pants. Eyes on hers, he redid his fly. "If you have our baby the two of you will be spending a lot of time here. And," he concluded happily, "I want you both to be comfortable."

OKAY, Maggie thought, still scolding herself silently some twenty five minutes later. It was way past time for her to get a grip on her out-of-control emotions, and increasingly vivid fantasies about their future. When Gabe had asked her to re-do the master bedroom of his beach house, he hadn't been proposing they turn their for-the-sake-of-the-baby marriage into a real one.

He hadn't been proposing anything even remotely close to that.

He was just thinking ahead to how they could best spend time with the baby they hoped they had already created. And yet the secret, romantic side of Maggie couldn't help but wish—however wistfully and un-realistically—that Gabe was at least showing some interest in taking their relationship to a deeper and more long-lasting level. Because more and more she was wanting just that.

"Everything okay?" Gabe asked curiously as they pulled into the doctors' parking lot at the hospital.

Realizing—too late—that she wanted a real family, with a mom, dad and kids, almost as much as she wanted a baby, Maggie nodded. "Sure," she said, doing her best to mask her tumultuous emotions and behave as confidently as possible. She turned to him with a dazzling smile. "Why wouldn't it be?"

Gabe shrugged his broad shoulders and continued to study her intently. "You've been pretty quiet."

"I was just thinking about Jane Doe," Maggie fibbed, her glance falling to his hands as he switched off the car, and pulled his keys out of the ignition. "Wondering how she is, and if she'll tell us who she is."

Gabe's dark brow furrowed hopefully. "One way to find out."

Together, they headed up to the fourth-floor nurses' station. They ran into Penny Stringfield just down the hall from Jane Doe's room. To Maggie's relief, the pretty young nurse looked more composed than she had the last time they had seen her. "Has anyone visited Jane Doe today?" Gabe asked.

"It's hard to say," Penny replied honestly. "We've been very busy today. There was a birthday party for one of the patients, so a lot of people were coming in and out for that."

Maggie did her best to curtail her disappointment. She had so hoped that a family member would have shown up to claim the sweet elderly woman by now. But maybe there were other choices, as well. "Did you see a young girl, about twenty, with freckles and long curly red hair walking around here today?"

"No, but again," Penny cautioned with a serious look at Maggie, "we've been really busy today so it doesn't mean she wasn't here. Why?"

Briefly, Gabe explained to Penny about the note that had been left by the mysterious jogger. "Hmm. Well, no one has called here," Penny said.

"Has anyone identified Jane Doe or given you any knowledge of her family?" Maggie asked hopefully.

"Nope." Penny sighed with mutual frustration. "Not a word."

"What about at the TV station?" Gabe pressed impatiently.

Penny frowned. "Lane hasn't called and he promised to let me know personally if they got any clues from the story they've been running."

Maggie looked at Gabe and saw he had the same hopes as she did for the estranged couple. "How are things going with Lane?" Gabe asked.

"Don't ask," Penny said, lifting her hand as if it were a stop sign.

"I was hoping—" Gabe said.

"We both were," Maggie added gently.

"I know." Penny flashed them both a wan smile. Suddenly she seemed near tears. "But I don't think he's going to forgive me."

"Oh, Penny." Maggie touched her arm gently.

Penny blinked back tears and offered up a brave

smile. "Listen," she said to them both, swallowing hard, "I've got to go. I'll ask around and let you know if anyone saw the red-haired girl." She rushed off.

Gabe went on to the nurses' station, where he picked up Jane Doe's chart and then he and Maggie proceeded down the hall to Jane Doe's room. Although the elegant older woman was still using nasal oxygen to help her breathe, she was sitting up in bed and reading the paper. Gabe looked over her chart, then said, "Looks like your fever is down. So is your white count."

"That's what they tell me," Jane Doe noted happily.

Gabe put his stethoscope in his ears and listened to her heart and lungs. As soon as he was finished, he told her, "If you keep improving at this rate, you might be able to go home in a few days."

Jane Doe looked from Maggie to Gabe and back again. "What about the two of you?" she asked impertinently. "Are the two of you going home together yet?"

Maggie's jaw dropped in surprise, even as she burst out laughing. As did Gabe. "Now Jane," Gabe scolded sternly, as he laced his stethoscope around his neck, "that's not very polite of you."

"I know what goes on with young people these days," Jane said, waving off Gabe's admonishment. "Things happen awfully quickly. There was a time when I didn't agree with that.'' Briefly, her eyes turned misty before she composed herself once again. ''Now that I'm older and I've wasted my own fair share of time, I think quicker and more impetuous might be smarter after all.'' She turned her hands palm up. ''After all, who knows what tomorrow is going to bring?''

Exactly, Maggie thought. Tomorrow, she might be pregnant. Tomorrow, Gabe might have already lost interest in her—again. Sometimes all you really had was today….

''I'm not sure our families would agree about that,'' Gabe said gently. ''And speaking of families…'' He reached into his pocket and withdrew the letter that had been left on Maggie's deck. He handed it over, an expectant look on his handsome face. ''What do you make of this?''

Jane Doe read the letter.

''*Do* you have a family?'' Gabe pressed.

''I'm very tired now,'' Jane Doe said, stubbornly refusing to answer Gabe's very direct query. She put her newspaper aside and lay back against the pillows. ''I think I'd like to rest.''

''If you do have a family,'' Maggie said gently, doing her best to convince Jane it was past time to trust someone to help her, ''and they really don't know about you, then it's probably time for you to notify them.''

Jane Doe turned her head to the side, away from

both Gabe and Maggie. "If I had a family," she said, tears sparkling in her eyes, "and they knew about me, I'm sure they would just want to put me in a nursing home. I'm not going to a nursing home."

"Do you know who the girl who left this note might be, then?" Gabe asked.

Maggie added, "She had long curly red hair and freckles. She was very pretty and very young. And she obviously cares about you very much."

For a heart-rending second, Maggie thought Jane Doe was going to confess something. Then she shut her eyes. "I can take care of myself," Jane Doe said firmly. "I've been doing so nearly all my life. The two of you just need to worry about your own romance. And nothing more."

ABLE TO SEE they had gotten as far as they were going to get in one hospital visit, Gabe and Maggie walked back out into the hall. "I wonder why she's so concerned about us," Maggie said, perplexed.

"I don't know." Gabe rubbed the back of his neck in obvious frustration. "I don't even know how she knows about us," he added, upset.

Maggie shrugged. "Well, we have visited her together several times."

Gabe's eyes darkened as he countered, "But we weren't holding hands or anything. For all anyone knows we could be just friends."

Wasn't that the truth? Maggie thought, dispiritedly.

Although the two of them had a marriage certificate and perhaps a baby on the way that said different. ''Maybe she's just intuitive,'' Maggie suggested after a moment, doing her best to hide the downward spiral of her mood.

''Maybe. One thing is for sure, though, as soon as her pneumonia is completely cleared up and she is well enough to be released, the hospital will insist we free up her bed. And if that happens and we still don't know who she is, Jane Doe will end up in the county nursing home—at least temporarily.''

In Maggie's opinion, Jane wasn't nearly ready for that. And hence wouldn't be happy there at all, sprained ankle or not. Maggie sighed as she shot a troubled look at Gabe. ''I don't want to see that happen.''

''Neither do I,'' Gabe commiserated gently, ''but I don't know what else we can do about it that we haven't already done.''

''Maybe Jane will change her mind and tell us more about the specifics of her situation the next time we visit,'' Maggie suggested hopefully.

''Maybe,'' Gabe said. He looked as if he were hoping for the same thing. ''Or maybe Harlan Decker, the private eye my aunt hired, will be able to identify her and track down her family.''

Down the hall, the elevator doors opened. Gabe's sister, Amy Deveraux, stepped out. Seeing them, she waved and came toward them. ''Hey there, big brother.'' Looking every bit the pampered baby girl of the Deveraux clan, the dark-haired Amy stood on tiptoe to kiss her older brother's cheek. Looking as glad to see her as she was to see him, Gabe hugged her back.

Amy smiled a tentative hello at Maggie, looked her over with frank curiosity, then drawled in a low confidence-inspiring tone, ''I heard the two of you were keeping company.''

Gabe immediately tensed.

Maggie understood why. Up until recently, no one in his family had wanted to see her and Gabe together—at all.

''Who from?'' Gabe snapped irritably, looking as if he didn't appreciate his sister's nosy attitude at all.

Amy grinned cheerfully. Sliding both her hands in the front of the lemon-yellow overalls embroidered with the logo for Amy's Cottage Redecorating, she rocked back on the heels of her sneakers and continued prodding her brother for details. ''Daisy Templeton mentioned it. She said nearly every time she comes over to take photos of the ongoing kitchen renovation at your place for Chase's magazine, that the two of you are there together.''

Able to see Amy's nosiness was getting under Gabe's skin, and for good reason, given how private a person he was, Maggie butted in, just as cheerfully. ''There's a reason for that,'' Maggie told Amy. ''He's my client. I need to talk to him about what we're doing.''

Unfortunately for both her and Gabe, Maggie noted, Amy wasn't buying that particular explanation.

''I don't think that's what Daisy meant,'' Amy said with a speculative grin.

Gabe glowered at Amy in a way that let her know his love life was not open to public—or even family—rumination. ''Yeah, well, maybe Daisy is reading too much into that,'' Gabe said, in a voice that relayed that his personal life was staying a closed book. He folded his arms in front of him and looked Amy up and down. ''What brings you here anyway?''

Amy sighed and put whatever interest or private reservations she might have had about Maggie and Gabe seeing each other aside. ''You remember I was a Lamaze coach a few months ago for that friend of mine whose husband is in the military?''

Gabe nodded, his look turning to one of approval. ''Lola had a boy, didn't she?''

''Yes.'' Amy grinned, recalling. ''Anyway, there's a 'class reunion' tonight, for the parents and their babies, and since Lola's husband Chuck is still overseas, I said I would come and be here with Lola and her baby, Dexter. But that's not why I was looking for you, Gabe.'' Amy grabbed him by the sleeve and stepped into the little hall, where snacks and beverages were kept for patients. Her expression became abruptly grim and worried as she leaned forward earnestly. "We have a family crisis."

IT WOULDN'T BE the first family crisis they'd had, Gabe thought. And it probably wouldn't be the last. He just didn't want to deal with it tonight—not when he was set to have another evening alone with Maggie. Not when—circumstances being favorable—they could get back to work on making that baby they both wanted so much. And making their relationship an enduring, instead of a temporary one.

But, as usual, his family was less concerned with what Gabe might want or need, than with what they needed and wanted.

Taking care to include a startled Maggie in the discussion, Amy continued anxiously. "Dad has a date tonight with some young thing."

"So?" Gabe shrugged his shoulders. For the life of him, he couldn't see what the big deal was about that. "Mom's been seeing a lot of that yoga instructor, Paulo."

Amy scowled, suddenly looking a lot younger and more naive than her twenty-eight years would warrant. "But Dad hasn't dated anyone since Mom has been back in town."

Hmm. That was new. Gabe narrowed his eyes at his sister. "You're sure about that?" he demanded.

"Yes," Amy retorted fiercely, her hope that their parents would one day reconcile unchanged. "But then Dad saw Mom with Paulo last night—we ran into them at the symphony concert—and he was furious. And I don't blame him. Paulo is half Mom's age. And with that long hair and fabulous body—well, it's no wonder Dad was ticked off!''

The last thing Gabe wanted to do was envision his mother with a man who was quite possibly the most popular yoga instructor-cum-ladies'-man in all of Charleston. He set his lips together firmly. ''It's really none of our business, Amy.'' And that would have been true even if his mother was involved with a gigolo, which—according to Gabe's usually pretty reliable sources—Paulo definitely was not.

''*Au contraire,* big brother, it is our business,'' Amy shot back, steam practically coming out of her ears she was so upset. Amy grabbed him by his necktie and admonished emotionally, while an astounded Maggie watched, ''This is our family we're talking about. And I'm not about to let Mom and Dad blow their chance to be together again. So I did something about it.'' Ignoring Gabe's groan of dismay, Amy released her death grip on his tie and continued, only slightly more calmly, ''I set up a fake emergency at the family yacht and I called both of them and left frantic messages. They should both be showing up there soon to rescue me. The only problem is I won't be there, of course, because I have to be here, at the Lamaze class party. So you'll have to show up in my place, Gabe, and reassure them that I'm all right.''

Gabe stared at his younger sister, not sure whether to haul her down to the yacht slip with him, or simply keep her as far away from both their parents as possible. "This is, without a doubt, the stupidest stunt you have ever pulled," he growled.

Amy flashed him a so-there! smile. "But I'm the baby of the family," she taunted in a low, irritatingly knowledgeable voice, "and they'll forgive me when they get back together."

Gabe rolled his eyes. "If they get back together," Gabe warned. He didn't think there was a chance on this green earth that they would.

"Positive thinking, Gabe. Positive thinking." Amy threw her arms around Gabe's neck, hugged him hard, and rushed off down the hall.

As soon as she was gone, Gabe and Maggie turned to each other. "So are you going to do it?" Maggie said, her face giving no clue as to what she was really thinking about.

"I have to," Gabe returned with the same grim reluctance he had used to witness his parents' split, "if I don't want Mom and Dad to go out of their minds with worry about Amy." He paused, raked both hands through his hair as the anxiety in him began to build. "I just hope they won't be too ticked off."

But of course they were ticked off—rightly so.

"What's going on?" Tom Deveraux demanded, the moment Gabe approached the slip where the family yacht, the *Endeavor,* was anchored. In a dark business suit and handsome tie, he looked every bit the successful, single CEO. Beside him was a young, sexy woman Gabe recognized as one of the docents at the Charleston Museum.

"Yes," Grace Deveraux rushed up to join them, Paulo by her side. The city's premiere yoga instructor was clad in an ivory silk shirt and trousers. He had his hand beneath Grace's elbow, steadying her, as the two navigated the weathered wooden dock next to the boat. As always, Gabe was surprised by how pretty his mom looked in a slim red silk sheath and matching pumps, her fluffy, short hair a halo about her head.

"Amy said there had been a break-in here, but I don't see any police," Tom growled.

Correctly sensing that he would like a little privacy with his parents, Maggie slipped away from Gabe and boarded the yacht, where she began to look around.

Grace's brow furrowed. "Amy's message to me stated she was having a crisis. I assumed she meant an emotional one."

"Relax," Gabe said, holding up a hand before his parents could stress out even more.

Acutely aware this was not a mess of his making, even if he had been left to clean it up, he went on to look his parents in the eye and admit uncomfortably, "There's no crisis. This was all a matchmaking ruse that Amy cooked up and put into motion." One meant to bring the two of them together in a romantic, happily-ever-after moment that Gabe was equally certain would never occur. Even if they locked the two of them in a room.

"Are you part of it?" Tom frowned.

Gabe shook his head, his mood increasingly grim and resentful at the awkward position he had been put in. "Only in that she sent me here to make sure you both knew she wasn't in any danger," he said quietly.

"Well, then where is she?" Grace demanded, looking just as incensed as Tom.

"At the hospital, attending a party for the Lamaze class she participated in a few months ago."

Grace and Tom both sighed—loudly. Not surprisingly, their dates looked increasingly uncomfortable, too.

Maggie came back down the gangplank. "If anyone is interested, there's a romantic dinner for two set up in the stateroom," she announced cheerfully.

"Well, I'm not staying," Grace said stiffly. She shot an angry look at Tom and his date.

"Neither am I," Tom said, wrapping his arm around his date's waist.

"If you see Amy tell her we did not appreciate this," Grace added over her shoulder as she took off with Paulo.

"And tell her it better not happen again," Tom seconded, as he and his date headed out in the opposite direction.

Gabe watched his parents go, then released a long,

pent-up breath as the tension began to ease out of him as swiftly and surely as it had come.

"Now what?" Maggie asked curiously.

Not about to waste a perfectly good opportunity to enjoy some time alone with Maggie, Gabe grinned and said, "Did the dinner look good?"

"I don't know." Maggie shrugged as color swept into her high, delicately boned cheeks. Her eyes met his in a welcoming glance. "I didn't lift the lids on the chafing dishes, but the flowers are fresh and the table is set beautifully."

That settled it then, Gabe thought. His sister Amy might have made things worse for their parents, but she had also made the situation better for him. His spirits lifting, Gabe took Maggie's hand in his and looked deep into her eyes. "It'd be a shame to let it all go to waste," he told her cheerfully. "Want to take the boat out?"

HERE IT WAS, Maggie thought, the big romantic evening she had been wanting. There was only one hitch. And it was a big one. Maggie hesitated, then admitted in a low, embarrassed tone, "I would love to, but I get seasick."

Gabe's eyes widened with the amazement Maggie would have expected from the scion of a shipping magnate and member of a sailing family. "You're kidding."

"Nope. Even a patch doesn't always work, so—"

she gazed at the sun setting over the harbor and tried not to think how lovely it would be to spend the night with Gabe out on the ocean somewhere. She withdrew her hand from his and released a wistful sigh. "I don't think I better try it."

"How about just staying here on the boat, then?" Gabe asked, looking as if he wanted nothing more than to make love to her then and there. He gently pushed an errant tendril of hair from her face. "Think you could handle that?"

Maybe there was a chance they could take this relationship of theirs to the next level after all. Maggie could hope anyway. She smiled back at him. "Probably."

As they headed to the stateroom below, Gabe's cell phone rang. He took it off his belt. "Ten to one that's Amy," he predicted to Maggie before he answered the insistent ringing. "How do you think it's going?" Gabe demanded in mounting exasperation as Maggie worked on opening the bottle of wine on the table. "They left—with their dates. And I have to tell you, kiddo, you're on the top of their hit lists." He paused and listened a moment, then continued in a much gentler tone. "I know. I've often wished our family could be whole again, too, but the harsh reality is that Mom and Dad *aren't* going to get back together. So just cool it with the matchmaking maneuvers, okay, little sis?" They talked a little more, then hung up. Gabe accepted the glass of wine Maggie handed him.

"Sorry you had to witness so much family drama in one evening," he said with a disgruntled sigh, looking as if he were weary of the whole Deveraux clan and all their various problems.

"I don't mind," Maggie said wistfully, as she took a sip of the delicious merlot. She let the mellow flavor rest on her tongue a moment before admitting in the same low shy tone, "Actually, I kind of miss having family crises like that."

"Were your parents passionate people?"

"Sometimes. Most of our family calamities were simply me being dramatic, and them reacting to me. But there were also times when they would have a disagreement, usually about something really silly and inconsequential, and want me to take sides."

Gabe made a face, letting her know he understood too well how it felt to be put in the middle of your parents' argument. "And did you?" he asked quietly, as they seated themselves on the long white leather sofa beneath the stateroom windows.

Maggie kicked off her high heels and curled up next to him. "Well, I always had an opinion about who was right and who was wrong and I think they kind of knew what I was thinking, even though I was careful to try not to get in the middle of whatever dispute they were having. What about you?" She traced his knee through the fabric of his stone-colored slacks. "Did you take sides when your parents got divorced?"

"I think we all did initially." Gabe took a sip of his drink and draped his arm along the back of the sofa. He turned to Maggie, so she was nestled in the curve of his arm, and continued in a soft reflective tone, "Chase sided with Mom. He didn't know what Dad had done, but he figured it had to be pretty bad if Mom wanted a divorce. Mitch thought Dad was the reasonable one, and that Mom was reacting emotionally—not logically. Amy didn't care who was at fault, she just wanted them to get back together."

"What about you?" Maggie asked gently, knowing he had to have been greatly affected, too.

Gabe shrugged, turned his glance away. His expression was bleak and brooding. "I was angry at both of them for letting whatever it was wreck our family. Back then, I believed in a perfect world." He shifted his gaze back to Maggie. "I knew our family wasn't perfect. There were a lot of stony silences. Locked bedroom doors. Hurt feelings. My father looked sad and angry. My mother just hurt and disillusioned. But I never once, in the months leading up to the divorce, thought they would ever forget the vows they had made to each other, or throw away the family that we had created."

But they had, Maggie thought sadly. And for all four of Tom and Grace Deveraux's offspring, the ramifications of that hurt were still resounding in their lives. Her heart going out to Gabe, she touched his

knee gently. "Do you think they could have saved their marriage?"

"I don't know," Gabe said honestly, the bitterness from years past coming back into his eyes. "What still bugs me, I guess, is that they didn't even try. Marriage is supposed to be for life."

Maggie stiffened. "Ours isn't," she reminded quietly. And for that, she would always have some regret. She knew now she never should have let him talk her into an in-name-only relationship, even if it was to keep their baby from feeling any shame about the way he or she had been created and or come into this world. She should have held out for the real thing or remained single. But it was too late to go back and do it all over now. They were in this farce together. And with Gabe as disillusioned as he apparently was about marriage in general, what hope did they have of ever making their union a true and lasting one? Maggie wondered wistfully. Even his parents—who had at least started out the right way—had failed in that regard.

Gabe put his wineglass aside. The next thing Maggie knew he had put hers aside, too, and shifted her over onto his lap. "You know what I mean," he said quietly, looking deep into her eyes.

Maggie laced her arms about his shoulders, for a moment allowing herself the luxury of sinking into his embrace. She loved the way he felt against her, so solid and warm and strong. "You're talking about marriages like my folks'," she observed quietly, wondering at how tenderly he treated her, as well as how protected, loved and at peace she felt whenever she was with him like this. She swallowed hard around the growing knot of emotion in her throat. "They really did have a wonderful partnership. So good, in fact," she reflected sadly, "that I sometimes worry if anything I have will measure up to the standard that they set."

Gabe sympathized, and more, understood. He reached out to cup her chin in his hand. "I have a feeling you're going to get what you want."

What she wanted, Maggie thought, was a real family. With a man who loved her—and the babies they had—for all eternity. But Gabe wasn't offering her that, she reminded herself sternly. Nor, given the in-name-only union they had embarked upon, was he ever liable to do so.

Chapter Ten

"Is that rain?" Maggie asked two hours later as she and Gabe finished doing the dishes in the narrow galley kitchen off the stateroom.

Gabe cocked his head in the direction of the whisper-soft sound above them. "Sure sounds like it," he mused, after a contemplative moment.

Maggie moved to the porthole to see for herself just as the clouds opened up. Big fat drops of water fell from the pitch-black sky in a pounding deluge on the deck. Maggie listened to the steady *rat-a-tat-tat* and considered just how damp they would get if they tried to make a dash to his sports car in that. *Pretty darn wet,* she figured silently. "That's a lot of rain," she noted. Not that she minded being here, in the lap of Deveraux family luxury with Gabe. There was something comforting and cozy about being inside the yacht's stateroom with him, while all manner of hell broke loose outside.

Gabe nodded, looking no more disturbed by the

unexpected tempest than she was. He wrapped his arms around her, testing the waters cautiously as he warned with a teasing grin, "If we go out in that, we'll get soaked."

The reckless part of Maggie wasn't sure that would be all bad. If their clothing was drenched, she'd get a better look at Gabe's strong, handsome physique. And there was no doubt about it. He had the build of an Adonis, with long limbs, beautifully sculpted muscles and a powerful chest. Lower still, he was just as beautifully and abundantly made.

Unfortunately, while the passionate side of her saw this as a perfect opportunity to make even more of her romantic fantasies come true with Gabe, Maggie's cautious side was throwing up the red flags. Before, she'd had good reason to take him into her heart and into her bed. Now, well, whether Gabe knew it or not, the situation was different. So different it was bothering her conscience.

Maggie sighed and stepped back slightly.

She looked back out the window and winced as a slash of yellow lit the sky. It was immediately followed by a clap of thunder so loud, it had her jumping right back into his arms. Embarrassed by the quick and instinctive way she had turned to him for protection, she flushed self-consciously and said, "Not to mention, possibly struck by lightning."

"Not to worry," he murmured, kissing her temple. Looking all too happy to be her white knight, whenever, however, she needed him, he flashed her a sexy smile. "I'll protect you."

Suddenly Maggie was shivering for a completely different reason. As much as she wanted Gabe to come to her rescue, she didn't want to be just another good deed in a long line of Good Samaritan pursuits. She curved her hands around the flexed muscles of his arms. It was late, and she was feeling far too vulnerable. "Gabe—"

Their gazes met, he regarded her in contemplative silence. "Hmm?" Not dissuaded in the slightest, he scored the pad of his thumb across her parted lips.

She hitched in a deep, galvanizing breath. "I'm not ovulating any more," she told him honestly, wanting—needing—him to know, before this sexy interlude really took flight.

His glance unexpectedly affectionate, and unrepentantly sensual, Gabe cupped her face ever so gently between his hands. "So?"

"So," Maggie elaborated, just as plainly, her low voice vibrating in the soft silence of the evening. Aware that with every touch, every passing moment, came the need to be so much closer, she looked deep into his eyes, and continued explaining tersely, "if we were to make love now, we wouldn't be making a baby." *And that was the only reason they had gotten married.*

Gabe smiled, apparently not the least bit upset

about that. "There are other reasons—even better reasons—for us to be together," he stated confidently.

Maggie's heart took a little leap at the blatant sensuality in his gaze. Oh, how she wanted to do what
he was so definitely encouraging and run wild with
him. Determined however, not to make the same mistake twice, and let herself dream, even for one crazy
moment, that he might be in this for the long haul
with her, she caught his hands and removed them
from her face. Then stepped back, slapped her hands
on her hips and squared off with him.

"Like what, for instance?" she asked.

Ignoring her contentious stance, he stepped closer
once again and anchored one arm about her shoulders,
the other about her waist. His lips came down on hers,
soft and sure. "Like the fact I want you in my life,"
he told her firmly.

"As what, exactly?" Maggie demanded in a low,
trembling voice as she tried not to give in to his
tender, evocative kiss.

Gabe pressed a kiss on her temple, another across
her cheek. "As everything," he replied gently, looking deep into her eyes once again. "A friend. The
mother of my child. My lover. My love."

All those things sounded wonderful to Maggie.
But, even though he had said them sincerely, he
hadn't uttered the one word she had yearned to hear—
he hadn't stated he wanted anything long-term, hadn't
indicated—in any way—that he wanted to make her

his wife in anything but name only. And without that...

Gabe had only to look at Maggie's face and feel the new resistance in her body to know he had screwed up with her once again.

Before Maggie could do more than take a galvanizing breath, Gabe swept her wordlessly into his arms, carried her resolutely across the hall, and set her down next to the bed.

"Stop fighting me, Maggie," he said. "Stop fighting this."

Her heart fluttered once in anticipation, then her lips were inundated with a kiss that was long and hard and deep, sweet and slow, soft and tempting.

She'd thought they could separate love and sex, baby-making from lovemaking, but as Gabe continued to kiss and caress her, for Maggie it all became one and the same. She couldn't make love to him without loving him. She couldn't have his baby without taking him into her life, into her heart. When she was in Gabe's arms like this, all she could think about—all she wanted—was to surrender to the feelings, the possibilities, the future. Their future.

It didn't matter that these lusty feelings were quite unlike her. Or that she had never behaved so wildly and wantonly in her life. All she knew for certain was that she wanted to be with him, and that the need deep inside her seemed to grow exponentially even as it was met. Standing on tiptoe, she returned his kisses passionately, knowing that no one had ever desired her in such a fundamental way. She shuddered as he swept off her jacket, her dress.

His eyes darkened as he took in her lacey lingerie, thigh-high stockings and heels. "Let yourself go, Maggie," Gabe whispered as he fell to his knees in front of her. He stroked the tender insides of her legs from knees to pelvis and back again, slid his fingers beneath the elastic of her panties, found and traced the dampness that flowed.

They'd barely started, and already she felt herself sliding inexorably to the edge. Not sure she could take much more, Maggie quivered and whispered, "Oh Gabe."

Gabe released a sound that was part chuckle, part groan and all male triumph. Holding her fast, he brought her even closer, pushed her panties down, off. Using the pads of his fingertips, he traced the satiny petals. Made lazy circles. Moved up, in. Followed it all with the soothing ministrations of his lips, coaxing response after response from her, until she was swaying against him mindlessly, aware of the need growing inside her, by leaps and bounds, even as it was met.

"I wanted to wait for you," she murmured, as he laid her gently back onto the bed.

"Not to worry," he murmured confidently as he stripped off his clothes—and hers—and lay down beside her. "I'll catch up." He was hard as a rock against her as he stretched out over top of her, took her wrists in his hands, pinned them over her head, making no bones about who was in charge. The softness of her breasts molded to the hardness of his chest, as her head swam with the scent and taste of him. Her abdomen felt liquid and weightless, her knees weak. The next thing Maggie knew, Gabe was claiming her body with the unchecked abandon they'd discovered the very first time they'd made love. Her heart was thumping so hard she could hear it in her ears as he kissed her over and over again. She wrapped her legs around him, reveling in the hot insistent demand, the deliberate thrust and parry. Sensations swept through her as she surged against him, taking him deeper and deeper inside her, closing tight, merging their bodies as intimately and intricately as they had begun to merge their lives.

Gabe had known that if they made love expressly to make love, it would change things, deepen their relationship. Which was, surprisingly enough, exactly what he wanted. Maggie in his life. Not just temporarily, or for a single reason—that reason being the baby they hoped they had already made—but forever. He could barely control himself as she moved against him. He heard her moan and felt her closing tight, and then it was just too much. He saw the tenderness in her eyes as she rose up to meet him. She arched her back, he plunged deep inside. And then they were one, in heart, soul, mind.

He was protecting her—even as they possessed each other. She was surrendering. Their joining was as tender as it was full of wonder. And somehow…it was exactly right.

MAGGIE WOKE on her side, with Gabe cuddled against her, his hand on her tummy. Loving the way he felt against her, so warm and strong and comforting, she put her hand atop his and snuggled even closer.

He kissed the curve of her bare shoulder, whispered in her ear. "I hope you're pregnant."

Maggie thought about the possibility of holding their baby in her arms nine months from now. Smiling, she murmured in reply, "I do, too."

Gabe rolled her ever so gently onto her back and lowered his mouth to hers. "But if not," he grinned down at her wickedly before kissing her so slowly and evocatively it set her body humming and her heart pounding, "I don't mind getting some more practice in." And to show her that was indeed the case, he made love to her all over again, every bit as sweetly and tenderly and erotically as he had the night before.

Afterward, they showered together, and took their time getting ready to face the day.

"Want to grab some breakfast before we head our separate ways?" Gabe asked, as Maggie finished dressing in the same outfit she had been wearing the night before.

Wishing they didn't have to resume their normal lives at all, Maggie nodded. Hand in hand, they headed up the companionway, to the deck of the yacht…and came face to face with Gabe's mother and father.

Gabe did a double take, as did Maggie. ''What are you two doing here?'' he asked, while Maggie gathered her composure around her like a cloak. It was clear Gabe's parents hadn't come for a happy reason. Both of them looked as ticked off as could be.

''This,'' Grace said, handing over a folded section of the *Charleston Bulletin* to her son.

Gabe looked down at the article she had circled in red.

''Deveraux Heir Takes Secret Bride,'' he read out loud.

Maggie glanced over his shoulder and continued where he left off. ''Dr. Gabe Deveraux married local kitchen designer Maggie Callaway in a private beachside ceremony in North Carolina earlier this week.''

''We don't even have to ask you if it's true,'' Grace said, as she studied their faces.

Tom nodded, just as grimly, and continued in a low voice laced with disappointment, ''We can tell by the looks on your faces that it is.''

Gabe edged closer to Maggie and put his arm around her waist. Although his action was casually possessive and protective, she could feel the tension thrumming through his body. ''How did you know we were here?'' Gabe asked his parents, while Maggie worked to get a handle on her own soaring emotions.

"Simple deduction,'' his father replied, giving Maggie a brief, assessing look that only intensified her guilt over having unintentionally caused even more havoc in the Deveraux family dynamics.

"We called both your homes,'' Tom continued briskly. "When we didn't get an answer we figured you must have spent the night here.''

"Why would you do something like this without even telling us either before or after?'' Grace cried, as she paced back and forth and wrung her hands.

"Marriage is not a game,'' Tom scowled, backing up his ex-wife in the same way Gabe was backing up Maggie. Which just went to show, Maggie thought, that chivalry ran rampant in the Deveraux family, no matter what the circumstances.

"I take my marriage to Maggie very seriously,'' Gabe said.

Tom looked at Maggie and assessed her bluntly. "What about you?'' he demanded impatiently. "How do you feel about this?''

Maggie drew a deep, calming breath, and edged even closer to Gabe. "Believe me,'' she told Gabe's father honestly, "I've never felt it was a more serious matter than I do right this very minute.''

Tom sighed, swept a hand through the short, cropped layers of his dark hair. "If you two are serious about each other and want to keep the tabloids from digging for scandal—''

He'd lost her, Maggie thought. ''Why would they be interested in the two of us?'' she interrupted. She wasn't a public figure. Neither was Gabe.

''Because of my celebrity,'' Grace explained unhappily. ''The fifteen years I spent as co-host on ''Rise and Shine, America!'' made me a very familiar face in this country. Since the network let my contract lapse, interest in my private life has only increased. And unfortunately, that includes both of you, too. If you two had said your vows in a long-scheduled church wedding, it probably wouldn't have been news. But the fact Maggie was once engaged to Chase, coupled with the fact that the two of you ran off to North Carolina to marry in secret…well, you can understand why the New York City newspapers jumped on the news. They've been wondering what I've been doing down here in Charleston while I was licking my wounds, and now they smell a juicy story. And where they go, the tabloids quickly follow.''

''We want to avoid a scandal at all costs,'' Tom said firmly.

''So do we,'' Maggie stated, just as fervently. The last thing she wanted to be was at the center of another Deveraux family scandal.

''Then we've got to embark on a P.R. offensive, fast,'' Grace said authoritatively, looking every bit the seasoned news professional that she was. ''And I have just the way to do it. Lane Stringfield's TV station is hosting the "Rupert and Casey Show" out of New York City. They are taping today's show live at 11:00 a.m. and I'm the first guest on the roster. I want you to go to the taping with me. And here's what we're going to do…."

"I'M NOT SURE I can do this," Maggie murmured to Gabe as Grace—finished with hair and makeup—was escorted off to do a pre-show interview with one of the staffers.

"Sure you can," Gabe said, as the two of them were ushered into the makeup chairs backstage. Looking handsome and sexy in a dark suit, light blue shirt and dark blue tie, he shot her a confident glance. "It's not hard at all. I did it all the time when I was growing up."

Trying hard not to think about how nice it would be to be a part of Gabe's life—and family—all the time, Maggie leaned forward so a protective cape could be slipped over her shoulders. She kept her back straight, her head up, as the stylist began touching up her hair with a curling iron. Catching Gabe's glance in the mirror, she smiled casually and asked, "What's it like being the kid of someone famous?"

Gabe made a face as the stylist working on him spread mousse through his black hair and finger-scrunched the thick layers so they would look even wavier. He turned his eyes to Maggie. "Being the offspring of a celebrity isn't really that different, except for times like this when I find myself in the limelight when I would rather not be.''

Maggie knew how Gabe felt. She'd rather be working on a remodeling job right now herself. Lane Stringfield walked past. He stopped when he saw Maggie and Gabe in the chairs, and came in. He looked at the makeup and hair artists working on them, and said with the polite authority of a TV station manager who had been in his job a long time, ''Give us a minute, would you please?''

They nodded and slipped out wordlessly.

Lane moved around to the front of the chairs. Although dressed as superbly as usual, he looked tired and stressed to the max. He leaned against the work counter, his back to the mirror. Folding his arms in front of him, he scowled at Gabe with unchecked resentment. ''Did you really expect me to forgive her?'' Lane asked.

Maggie didn't have to ask who Lane was talking about—it couldn't have been anyone but his estranged wife, Penny.

Abruptly, Gabe looked as grimly upset as Lane. ''If you love your wife,'' Gabe ground out, ''then yes, that is exactly what I would expect you to do.''

A mixture of hurt and indignation glimmered in Lane's eyes. ''She was unfaithful to me,'' he said.

''Nearly unfaithful,'' Maggie corrected, just as hotly. For reasons she didn't quite understand, she wanted the Stringfields to get back together, too. ''And given the fact Penny was very young at the time and targeted by a real pro, I'd think you would cut her some slack.'' Maggie knew what it was like to make mistakes. To look back and wish you had handled a situation differently. For instance, if she had kept her attraction to Gabe to herself at the time she broke up with Chase, she might have been able to see Gabe later, without all the subsequent family angst and complications. Instead, she had worn her heart on her sleeve in the days before her wedding to his brother Chase, and caused a Deveraux family uproar that had left the two brothers barely speaking, and Gabe and herself feeling so guilty and confused they had decided not to keep seeing each other after all.

Now, of course, she and Gabe were married, but it was more a business arrangement for the sake of the baby they were currently trying to have together than an actual union of souls. And to make matters worse, today, because of his mother's celebrity and his father's inherited wealth and social position within the community, they were having to pretend to all the world they meant more to each other than they had ever promised they would.

''I helped Penny go to the police and make a report,'' Lane countered. ''Which in turn caused the louse to leave town, and I hope he never comes back.'' Lane glared at Gabe and Maggie, before continuing flatly, ''That's all I'm prepared to do.''

He stalked out.

Maggie looked at Gabe. Her pulse had quickened, and she felt even more on edge. ''Do you think we made a mistake telling Penny to be honest with her husband?'' she asked cautiously.

Gabe shook his head. ''Lane is the one making a mistake,'' Gabe said firmly.

The hair and makeup people came back in. When Gabe and Maggie were all set, tiny microphones were clipped onto their lapels, and they were led to the front row of the audience and seated on the center aisle. A local comedienne came out to warm up the audience with a series of jokes. Before Maggie knew it, she was as relaxed as everyone else.

Then the countdown began. The music started, the hall lights dimmed, and the stage lights came up.

The sixty-something Rupert walked out, looking as dapper as always in one of his signature suit-and-tie ensembles. He was followed by Casey, his much younger prettier female co-host. For the first two minutes of the show, Rupert and Casey welcomed their audience and spoke enthusiastically about doing the show live in five different southern cities that week. Then they previewed the guests ahead and cut to commercial. Next up was Grace.

Maggie's nerves came back, full-force. She reached over and took Gabe's hand. Her palm was damp. His was warm and dry. He squeezed her hand reassuringly and leaned over and whispered in her ear. "You're going to be fine. Remember, all we have to do is wave and smile and look like happy newlyweds."

Maggie nodded, taking strength from his steady presence. It would be over in a minute. All she had to do was let Gabe help her through her first appearance on TV. It really didn't matter that Rupert and Casey had an audience of millions—or that she was so jittery she wanted to drop through the floor and disappear!

The show was back. Live. The first guest of the day was introduced and Grace Deveraux came out on stage to thunderous applause. Before they realized it, Maggie and Gabe were on their feet along with everyone else, clapping heartily for the newswoman who had been a part of so many Americans' morning routines for so many years.

"So I understand you've moved back to Charleston," Rupert began as soon as they were all seated again.

Grace nodded and smiled, looking remarkably content. "It is my home, after all," she said, smiling broadly.

"Your family is here."

"Right. All four of my grown children live right here in the Charleston area."

"And speaking of family," Rupert leaned over to pick up a copy of a newspaper from the low table in front of them, ''I understand one of your sons and his new bride have quite a story to tell.''

Oh, drat, Maggie thought, her heart sinking clear to the floor once again. *Here we go.*

''A happy story,'' Grace smiled. She turned to the audience and cheerfully imparted, ''My son Gabe eloped with Maggie Callaway earlier in the week.''

Rupert took a drink of his coffee. ''I take it you and your ex-husband were surprised,'' he noted with confidence-inspiring ease.

Grace nodded, still holding her own with the gregarious host. ''The whole family was caught off-guard. But it was a happy surprise.''

''I understand Gabe and Maggie are in the audience,'' Rupert said.

''Yes.'' Grace smiled and pointed them out.

''Let's get a camera on them, shall we?'' Rupert said.

As soon as they did, the stage director nodded at them—and Gabe and Maggie smiled and waved. Maggie breathed a sigh of relief. Her moment of national fame was over.

Or was it? she wondered, as Rupert stood and gestured toward them. ''Come on up here, you two lovebirds, and join your mom.''

Maggie froze and shot a panicked look at Gabe. This had not been part of the bargain. They were not supposed to have to leave their seats in the audience. ''Just go with it,'' he murmured, as they were egged on by thunderous applause and the continued cheer-leading of cohosts Rupert and Casey. What choice did she have? None, apparently. Her legs feeling like rubber, Maggie let herself be led up onto the stage. Two tall stage chairs were brought out for them to sit on, and placed between Grace and Rupert and Casey. "So tell us, you two," Rupert began with a wicked smile, "What made you two kids run off and do this in secret instead of having a normal family wedding?"

Grace placed a hand across her heart and inter-rupted with unabashed sentimentality, "I thought it was romantic."

"So, obviously, did we." Gabe shot a grateful smile at his mother for the save.

Undeterred in his quest to ferret out a little more info, Rupert turned his attention back to Grace. "You're the mother of the groom. Are you sorry there was no big wedding?"

Grace dropped her hand back to her lap and lifted her slender shoulders in a delicate shrug. "I can't deny it. I would have liked to see the wedding. But on the other hand, I've always tried to live by the credo, to each his own. And I have two other sons—Chase and Mitch—and I recently attended both their weddings. But—" Grace paused to shoot Maggie and Gabe an affectionate glance before turning back to Rupert and the audience and finishing sincerely "—mostly, I just want Maggie and Gabe to be happy, and if having a very romantic seaside elopement is what they wanted then…more power to them.''

The audience burst into spontaneous applause, agreeing with Grace's unanimous show of support.

Maggie could tell, however, from the determined gleam in his eyes that Rupert wasn't done trying to extract some juicy detail of some sort from them that would land clips of his late-morning talk show on news programs around the country.

"So, how long have you two been seeing each other, Maggie?'' Rupert asked her, even more cheerfully.

"We've known each other for several years,'' Maggie allowed uneasily, praying Rupert would let it go at that.

But of course, he didn't.

Rupert's brows knit together. As the cameras zoomed in for a close-up, he looked at Maggie, perplexed. "You were once engaged to Gabe's older brother, Chase, weren't you?''

Maggie swallowed as Gabe reached over and draped his arm around her shoulders in an open show of support. Gabe looked at Rupert steadily. "That didn't work out.''

Casey leaned in again. Her pretty eyes said she was full of sympathy for Maggie, and irritated at Rupert for sabotaging them. "You look very happy now,'' Casey said.

"I am. Very." Maggie smiled as her nervousness

increased and her heartbeat kicked up even more. *And I'll be even happier when I get off this stage.*

"YOU CAN STOP shaking now," Gabe said, as he led Maggie out to the restricted area where his car was parked. Inside the auditorium, the show was still going on, but, wary of being waylaid by the local press for more questioning about their romance and surprise nuptials after the show, Gabe and Maggie had sneaked out through the service entrance during a commercial break.

Maggie turned to Gabe as they walked across the crowded parking lot. Although their time in the spotlight had ended a good fifteen minutes earlier, her cheeks were still flushed a bright pink and her light-green eyes sparkled with agitation. Still studying him warily, she raked her teeth across her lower lip, and swallowed hard before continuing in a low, distressed tone, "That didn't get to you at all, did it?"

Gabe slid his hand beneath her elbow, and tucked her in closer to his side as they maneuvered between the rows. "I told you," he said, as they stopped next to his sports car. "I'm used to it."

"Well, I'm not." Maggie tucked her arms against her waist and turned her eyes away as she waited for him to unlock her door. "I hated lying that way."

Gabe helped her inside, then went around and climbed in behind the wheel. He shut the door, switched on the ignition. There was a two-second delay, then the air conditioner began to blow warm air into the interior of the car. Wanting there to be no distraction between them as they had this very important conversation, he switched off the radio, draped his right arm across the length of both bucket seats, and turned to her. Glad Rupert and Casey and the rest of the studio audience—never mind his family—could not see them now, he observed quietly, "You're not at all happy with the way that went, are you?" He thought, under the very dicey circumstances, it had turned out rather well.

"How can I be?" Maggie shut her eyes briefly and huddled miserably in her seat. "We made everyone think ours was a *real* marriage."

Gabe reached over with his left hand and touched her arm gently, offering what physical comfort he could in what was still a pretty public place. "Ours *is* a real marriage," he countered practically.

"Maybe in a legal sense," Maggie shot back in a low, cantankerous voice.

In every sense, Gabe thought. At least it had become so to him.

And last night, on the yacht, he had *thought* she had felt the same way. Had he been wrong about that? Once again reading more into her actions than was actually there?

"We're not even living together," Maggie continued her tirade, upset.

That was a problem they could fix, Gabe thought.

He curved his right arm closer about her shoulders and slipped his left hand down to twine with hers. "That's about to change," he said, his mood tense but hopeful.

Maggie went very still. The color in her cheeks deepening, she looked at him apprehensively. "What do you mean?" she whispered.

Gabe shrugged. He wished there weren't a gear box between them—so he could take her onto his lap. In any case, this had to be said. Practically, he explained, "The surest way to get a whole posse of tabloid press after us would be to take up separate residences. For both our sakes, for the baby's and for my mother's sake, we have to live together from here on out."

Maggie took a deep breath that lifted her breasts against the soft silk of her dress, releasing it just as slowly. Oblivious to what she was doing to him, with just her presence, she said, "We don't even know if I'm pregnant."

"We can hope," Gabe said as a silence fraught with emotion fell between them.

Because if she wasn't, Gabe wasn't sure how much longer Maggie would be willing to continue living under the public scrutiny that came with being his wife, and the daughter-in-law of celebrity Grace Deveraux.

Chapter Eleven

"I thought I might find you here," Gabe told Maggie, when he finally caught up with her.

Despite the fact she must hear the irritation in his low voice, Maggie didn't so much as look up from the ceramic tiles she was laying along the backsplash. Wearing paint-splattered jeans, a form-fitting pink T-shirt and an open blue chambray men's work shirt that hung nearly to her knees, her hair caught in a low ponytail on the back of her neck and tucked beneath a bill cap that sat backward on her head, she kept right on working as meticulously as ever.

"I've been looking for you for two hours," Gabe said grumpily.

"Hmm." Maggie continued working intently.

Teeth clenched, Gabe loosened and removed his tie and thrust it down on the newly installed marble kitchen counter beside Maggie. "We were supposed to talk at six, and decide where we were going to stay tonight, your place or mine."

This time, to his satisfaction, she did look at him.

She put down the tile she was holding. Straightened and planted both hands on her hips. Her pretty chin lifted as she squared off with him. "You want to flip for the sofa—is that it?" she inquired politely.

Gabe moved close enough to smell the hyacinth in her perfume, and—wanting there to be no misunderstanding about this—stated firmly, "No one is sleeping on the sofa."

Heightened color swept her cheeks. She shot him a mutinous look and muttered cantankerously, "Says you."

Gabe had known his family's money and/or his mother's celebrity would become an issue for them some day. He just hadn't expected her not to be able to blow it off, the way he always did. And even if they had fought about it, he had expected them to make up readily. Given the chill in her attitude, she wasn't planning on doing either anytime soon.

"What's that supposed to mean?" Gabe demanded, finding without warning that he was just as piqued as she was.

Maggie's soft lips pursed. She glared at him, her every defense against him suddenly in place. "It means suddenly you're pretty bossy and I don't like it," she spelled out plainly.

Gabe inclined his head right back at her. "Well, I don't like having to hunt all over heck for my wife," he said.

Maggie picked up another painted tile and bending across the counter, set it carefully in place. "No one asked you to do that," she reminded in a low, chilly voice that meshed perfectly with the damp fog rolling in off the ocean.

Finding it suddenly chilly, Gabe went over to shut one of the windows. "How come you're working here all alone tonight?" he asked curiously.

Maggie reached for another tile. Her focus completely on her work, she set it, too. "Because Enrico, Manuel and Luis all went home at six to have dinner with their families."

Gabe's stomach growled hungrily, reminding him he hadn't had dinner, either. "Are they coming back tonight?"

"No," Maggie replied stoically.

Despite himself, Gabe began to admire the way she was laying out the tiles, and the beautiful pattern she was making, as she alternated painted and plain tiles. "Then why don't you knock off, too?" Gabe asked curiously.

Maggie shot him a quelling look as she straightened once again. "Because I have a deadline to meet and contractual responsibilities to my clients," she explained impatiently.

Gabe shrugged and leaned back against the opposite counter. "I don't care if you finish this kitchen later than you said you would."

Maggie whipped off her baseball cap and slapped it against her thigh in aggravation. "But I care."

Gabe focused on the agitated light in her green eyes. "Why?"

Maggie smoothed a palm across the top of her head where the hat had sat, and finding it too rumpled to fix easily, frowned unhappily. "Because if I'm late on your job, then I'm going to be late on the next job, and because I was at the TV show taping with you this morning, I didn't even get started on my work here until around two this afternoon. Which means," she said, as she removed the elastic band around her ponytail with a snap, "I need to work until at least eleven tonight, just to stay behind. So, if you don't mind," she said grumpily, as she combed her honey-blond hair with her fingertips and then put it up in a ponytail once again, "I'm going to keep going until I finish with this backsplash."

Gabe straightened and moved away from the counter before she could turn away. "Which will be eleven?" he inquired calmly.

"Could be later." Maggie slapped her baseball cap back on her head, this time putting the brim over her eyes. "It's all taking longer than I estimated."

Gabe moved to block her way. "Then why not knock off and pick it up tomorrow?" he asked pleasantly.

Maggie reached around him for another unopened packet of ceramic tile. "I'd prefer to keep going."

His patience fading with remarkable speed, he watched her cut across the plastic seal. "And I'd prefer you to spend time with your family."

Maggie shot him a contentious look from beneath the shadowed brim of her ball cap. "What family?"

Gabe edged closer still. "Me."

Maggie tipped her chin at him. "We're not a family yet."

He smiled insincerely, not the least bit put off by the challenging lilt to her voice. "Then what am I to you?" he asked softly, succinctly.

"In reality?" Maggie contemplated, then said, "Potentially, the father to my child."

As if that were something to be discounted, Gabe thought, resentfully. "And husband," he reminded mildly.

"Only in the strictest legal sense," Maggie corrected with an arch lift to her brow. "Not in any real way."

Okay, Gabe thought. So maybe he deserved that one. Because the truth was, he had known from the outset that he wanted Maggie as more than just a friend, or a lover or even the mother to his child. He had wanted her to be his woman, heart and soul. He just hadn't thought it would ever be possible, given the entanglements of the past. But that had been before she had turned to him in time of crisis, in lieu of anyone else. Before she had agreed to have a baby with him and marry him, before she had made love

with him as if there was no other man for her and
never would be. He wasn't going to pretend none of
that had happened. And he wasn't about to let her
pretend they hadn't found something special, either.

"Obviously, you're ticked off at me," he stated,
after a moment.

Maggie studied him, silently assessing and deciding, Gabe figured, whether or not she should get any
further emotionally involved with him. He wanted her
to feel she could. He figured she had to know, somewhere deep inside her, that he had never wanted their
nuptials to become fodder for the media. And, in fact,
would have done whatever necessary to make sure
they didn't. He just hadn't foreseen anyone finding
out about their elopement to North Carolina before
they were ready to disclose it, and neither had she.

"I guess I am," Maggie agreed reluctantly at last.

Assured of her attention, he stood beside her and
asked, "Mind telling me why?"

Maggie grimaced in aggravation. "I don't like being trapped into doing things against my will." She
grabbed the bucket of cement and stirred it vigorously
as she continued, "I had enough of that when I was
a kid."

"What are you talking about?" Gabe demanded as
he watched her spread some more adhesive on the
wall above the counter. "I thought you had a happy
childhood."

"I did!" Maggie smoothed it in place with even strokes of her trowel.

Gabe tore his eyes from the faint jiggling motions of her breasts beneath her soft cotton T-shirt. This was no time to be thinking how well she filled out her clothes, he reminded himself sternly. He stepped back slightly to allow her room to work. "Then…?"

"I didn't always have choices." Finished, Maggie put the bucket and trowel aside and wiped her hands on a cloth, before throwing it aside, too. "I want choices."

Gabe watched her lay another plumb line across the bond with chalk and string, before starting up again. "In what way didn't you have choices?" he asked.

Maggie leaned across the counter to lay the first tile with the careful precision of an artist. Finished, she released a beleaguered sigh and reached for another tile. "From the time I was old enough to know the different types of cabinets and countertops and flooring, it was expected that I would keep Callaway Remodeling and Construction going."

Gabe watched her continue the pattern she had started, alternating plain and painted tiles. "I thought you loved your work."

Maggie stepped back to admire what she had done thus far. Her pouty lower lip curled thoughtfully as she propped her hands on her hips and looked at the half-tiled backsplash in front of her. "I love aspects of it. But—'' she turned to give Gabe an arch look ''—I might have loved something else as much or more, but I wasn't given the chance to explore my options and figure out what I wanted because of the demands of my family.'' Their eyes met and she shook her head unhappily, recalling. ''The needs of the business, and the expectations of my family overrode any choices I might have had.''

This, Gabe hadn't expected. He had always assumed, as did everyone else who knew Maggie, that she had never even considered doing anything else. He studied the unhappiness in her eyes, and wished, once again, that he could erase any and all negatives in her life.

''That might have been true while your parents were alive,'' he pointed out calmly, wanting her to take charge of whatever she could. ''But since your folks died and you inherited the business, you've made plenty of changes, concentrating on kitchens, which are your forte and turning down a lot of the other work.'' She also could have chosen to sell the business—she hadn't.

Maggie sighed heavily. ''That's not the point.''

''Then what is the point?'' Gabe studied the flushed color in her cheeks and the cautious sparkle in her green eyes.

Maggie threw her arms up in frustration and went back to laying tile, one by one. ''I thought I was free of arbitrary familial expectations and demands. And

now here I am again,'' she muttered grumpily, ''expected to move in with you by your family, because
your mother is a celebrity, and there's enormous public interest in her and her family life.''

Gabe moved around to stand beside Maggie, making sure he gave her plenty of room to work. Reminding himself to put her needs and wants ahead of
his own, despite what his own heart was urging him
to do, he told her matter-of-factly, ''You don't have
to move in with me.'' If she really wanted another
solution, they could find it. They just needed time.
And, he added dryly to himself, a little cooperation
from her.

Maggie made sure the patterned tile she was laying
was precisely in place, then turned to shoot him an
aggrieved look. ''If I don't, people will wonder
why,'' she explained irritably. She propped her hands
on her hips and angled her chin up at him contentiously. ''The little dog-and-pony show we put on
during the 'Rupert and Casey Show' will all be for
naught, because the tabloid press will start investi-
gating us. And then they'll find out about my visits
to the fertility clinic, and your no-show, and my fury,
and before you know it, the tabloids will be publish-
ing stories that our marriage is all a sham.''

To Gabe's chagrin, Maggie had a point. ''Then
there's only one way to fix it,'' he decided, just as
firmly. Stepping forward, he closed the distance be-

tween them, not stopping until they stood toe to toe. "We make our marriage a real one, in every way."

MAGGIE STARED at Gabe, not sure whether she wanted to hug him or throttle him. She only knew he was, without a doubt, the most persistently chivalrous man she had ever met in her entire life. The only problem was, she didn't want to be made his "wife" out of an act of mercy. It was bad enough they had decided to make their baby the old-fashioned way, and then kept right on making love to each other even after her fertile period had apparently passed. She'd told herself at the time it was simply lust, and the need to feel close to someone—physically and emotionally—in this very special time in her life that had driven her back into Gabe's arms, but in retrospect, she knew it had been a great deal more than that. She had made love with him again, because she was *in love* with him, and wanted him to be *in love* with her. But that wasn't going to happen, she schooled herself firmly, because true love wasn't something that could be ordered up on demand to make their lives work out more neatly. True love either happened or it didn't, and thus far, with Gabe, it simply hadn't.

Aware he was waiting for her response to his suggestion that they make their marriage a real one in every sense—except the spiritual, which couldn't be feigned, even by the hardiest Good Samaritan on earth—Maggie swallowed hard and looked Gabe straight in the eye. "And you know what I wish?" she lobbed back as she went back to what she was doing, laying the last of the patterned tiles on the diagonal she had carefully measured out. "I wish you wouldn't make our situation any more complicated than it already is."

"I'm not," he retorted, just as resolutely, as he moved in. An instant later, her back was to the counter and he was standing directly in front of her, his hands braced firmly on either side of her. "I'm talking about simplifying things—to the point that you would no longer have to hide from me."

Okay, so that was what she was doing. Did he have to be so ungentlemanly as to point it out? Maggie wondered silently as he caged her body with the taller, stronger, warmer length of his. She tipped her head back and intensified her glare. "Don't you need to go and eat some dinner or something?" she asked, doing her best to remain immune to the take-no-prisoners look in his eyes.

A knowing smile curved his lips. He leaned down and pressed kisses along her temple. "We both should eat some dinner," Gabe said.

Maggie watched the broad muscles strain against the fine cotton of his pale-green dress shirt and re-called without warning how good it felt to be envel-oped in their seductive warmth. Her breath caught in her throat, her heart beat wildly in her chest, and her head tipped back all the more. "I don't want to do that until I finish here," she told him defiantly.

"Fine," Gabe said, as he dropped kisses along the shell of her ear, and buried his face in her neck. "Then I'll help."

Aware she was weakening and he hadn't even kissed her—really kissed her—yet, Maggie splayed her hands across his chest. She hitched in a quick, bolstering breath. "You don't know what to do."

Gabe shrugged his broad shoulders amiably. "So show me."

"No," Maggie retorted stubbornly, knowing if she gave this man an inch, he would definitely take a mile, and then some.

Gabe drew back slightly. His eyes widened in surprise. "Why not?"

"Because," Maggie fibbed as she tried to quickly build a case against them spending any more time together, intimate or otherwise, "you're an amateur. And my company only does the most professional work."

Gabe paused and moved his torso in even closer, until his lower half rested against hers, and she could feel the depth of his arousal. "So teach me," he said softly, looking straight into her eyes. "I'm capable of learning."

Exactly what she was afraid of, Maggie thought. She didn't want him knowing any more about how to handle her. Not when she was this vulnerable to him already. "No," she replied, just as stubbornly.

"Okay, then," Gabe said, as she started to step past. He slid an arm beneath her knees, another behind her back. The next thing Maggie knew she was cradled against his chest and he was headed out of the kitchen, up the stairs to the master bedroom.

Cradled against his hard chest that way, she felt a little dizzy and out of breath, not to mention excited. Definitely excited. "Now what are you doing?" she demanded, as if she hadn't a care in the world.

He regarded her with a mixture of heat and tenderness that set her blood to racing as he charged into his bedroom, used the back of his wrist to turn on the lights, and set her down on the floor. "Time for bed."

Maggie swallowed around the sudden dryness of her throat and did her best to look as if she had little interest in making love with him again, when she knew darn well nothing could be further from the truth. "Says who?"

He grinned and gave her body a long, thorough once-over before returning his hot-blooded gaze to hers. He offered up a rapacious smile that promised untold delights as he told her softly, "Says your husband, that's who."

She ignored his teasing as her heart began to race. Shaking her head at him in mocking censure, she drawled in a voice that had no room for compromise,

"Very funny. I want to go home." *Before I fall even deeper in love with you.*

Gabe stepped closer, looking impossibly handsome and impossibly determined in the soft lamplight of his bedroom. "Not until you tell me one thing. What's it going to take to make this a real marriage?"

Love, Maggie thought. *I need you to love me the way I've started to love you.* But since that wasn't ever going to be the case.... "It can't ever be a real marriage," she said stubbornly, knowing feelings weren't something you could conjure up on demand.

Gabe's lips took on a tempting curve as he closed the distance between them, bringing a higher level of romance and tenderness into her life. "Tell me that again after we've made love," he murmured in a low sexy voice that stirred her passion, "and I'll believe you."

Anchoring an arm about her waist, he dipped his head, and caught her lips against his in a fierce, burning kiss that prompted her to answer his ardor with her own. Their tongues mated in an erotic dance unlike anything she had ever imagined and for the first time all day, Maggie realized she was exactly where she wanted to be. His arms were strong and protective, wrapping her in sensual pleasure, lower still there was a provocative hardness, heat and strength. And just as before, he knew exactly how to get to her as he molded her breasts with his hands, circled the aching crowns, teased her nipples into tingling awareness.

Maggie moaned low in her throat and moved closer yet. Gabe murmured his pleasure, then drew back a little, altering the angle, increasing the depth and torridness of their kiss. Her excitement mounted as he led her over to the bed. Finding her knees suddenly too weak to hold her, Maggie dropped down onto the edge of the bed. He knelt in front of her, and began untying the laces of her work boots. Needing to do something—anything—to maintain her dignity, even as he stripped off her work shirt, T-shirt and jeans, Maggie said, ''This proves nothing.''

Gabe let her clothes fall to the floor, then moved in between her knees. He looked up at her, his gray-blue eyes shimmering with a passion, want and need that matched her own. ''It proves you want me,'' he said softly.

She hitched in a deep trembling breath as he kissed his way up her thighs, past the triangle of golden curls, to her tummy. ''I never said I didn't,'' she asserted in a low trembling voice.

''True,'' he murmured, as he cradled her hips and thighs as if she were the most precious thing in the world and found her with his lips. His tongue plunged between the satiny folds, her head fell back. Her body shivered with exquisite need, and then she came apart in his hands, delicious tremors of pleasure ricocheting inside her.

Gabe held her until the aftershocks subsided. Ready to make her his, he stripped off his clothes, too. But Maggie, no passive woman in work and certainly not in play, wasn't ready for that.

She stripped back the covers, guided him to the pillows and straddled the length of his tall, strong body. Gabe grinned as she kissed her way down his chest, lingering over the hard pectoral muscles and tight abs before finding the flat male nipples with her fingers and tongue. He sucked in his breath as she moved lower still, to the throbbing hardness of his arousal. Senses swimming with the clean, musky scent of him, Maggie traced the hot, velvety skin, learning how to pleasure him with lips and teeth and tongue, until he was wanting her as much as she had wanted him, until he groaned and caught her head with his hands.

''Enough,'' he said in a low, gruff voice, turning her so she was beneath him. ''I want to be inside you.''

Heart soaring, Maggie accepted the warm, wonderful weight of him over top of her. ''I want that, too,'' she murmured, loving the way he felt as he fit the hard planes of his body to the softer dips and curves of hers.

He parted her knees with his, settled deeply between them, then his lips were on hers once again and his hands were sliding beneath her, lifting and positioning her. She felt his manhood poised to enter her.

She opened for him, like a flower blossoming in the spring, and then he plunged inside her, taking her completely, making it an all-or-nothing proposition with each slow, sexy stroke of his body. The climax she had felt earlier came roaring back in a rush of heat. She dug her fingers into his back and moved her hips to his commanding rhythm until a cry of exultation rose in her throat and was echoed in his. And then they were both soaring, wanting—finding—all they had ever dreamed possible in this crazy, mixed-up arrangement they called a marriage.

"YOU NEVER ANSWERED my question," Gabe said, an hour later, as they sat outside on the deck, enjoying the warm spring evening and a glass of wine, and waiting for the delivery of their dinner.

"What question?" Maggie asked, looking ravishingly beautiful in a pair of his boxers and one of his shirts.

Although Gabe knew he risked ruining their mellow mood, he also knew the two of them were never as close as they were immediately after making love. If they were going to go past the boundaries they had initially set and be closer still, he was going to have to push the envelope, and take his chances that Maggie would respond the way he wanted. Gabe exhaled slowly and continued to study her in the soft glow of outdoor lighting. "What's it going to take to make this a real marriage?" he asked. "You never answered me before."

Maggie shrugged and sent him a cautious smile. Abruptly, she was her old sassy self—pragmatic to a fault. "You tell me," she said softly, meaningfully, as yellow headlights swept the carport beneath the deck and a car pulled into his drive.

His heart began to beat like a bass drum. Reminded of all that was at stake here, Gabe promised, "I will tell you—in just one second."

Gabe hustled down the steps to meet the delivery person at the bottom of the stairs. He paid the guy, giving him a handsome tip, then carried the bag back up the steps and over to the patio table where Maggie was sitting. Her hair was tousled, both from their lovemaking and from the evening breeze, her cheeks were pink with emotion, her green eyes glittering expectantly. She looked edgy and kissable—and every bit as wary of messing up their "marriage" as he felt. And—like him—she seemed determined to take charge of what she could.

"Tell me something, Gabe," Maggie said, as he put the sacks onto the table in front of them. "What do you want from a wife?" Maggie sniffed appreciatively as the delicious aroma of Chinese food mingled with the fresh salt air.

Glad she was taking such an open-minded, practical approach, Gabe handed Maggie a set of chopsticks and laid out another for himself. Maybe there was a chance they could work this out yet, he thought hopefully. "Actually, a lot of things," he said.

Maggie shot him a curious look as she opened up the white cardboard containers of sweet and sour chicken and steamed rice. "Such as…?"

Sitting back in his chair, Gabe decided to start where they were having the most success. "Great sex, and lots of it."

Maggie grinned and admitted with the combination of sweet sensuality and shyness that had been driving him wild, in bed and out, "I think we've got that much covered."

Wanting her to know how deeply he felt about her now, and always would, Gabe looked at her in a way that let her know he was far from wiped out on that score. "I could make love to you all day and all night, and still never get enough."

Maggie blushed as she opened the beef and broccoli and handed it to him. "What else do you want from a wife?" she asked, as her fingers brushed his.

That, Gabe thought, wishing their evening together would never end, was easy. "A baby—our baby."

Maggie ducked her head shyly. "If we get our wish, we'll have that, too." She paused, bit her lip, some of the worry coming back into her eyes. "But it takes more than great sex and a baby to make a marriage, Gabe."

Gabe wanted to put their food aside, take Maggie into his arms, and make love all over again, until the love and passion were back in her eyes, and none of the doubt. But he knew doing that would only put off the inevitable. There were things they needed to talk about, he reminded himself firmly. The time was now, while they were alone. "I want to be able to talk to my wife, the way I can talk to you, and know she'll understand me, the way you understand me," he said softly.

"What about friendship?" Maggie asked, leaning over to pour them both some more wine.

Gabe grinned as he helped himself to more rice. "It's on the must-have list, too." And there was no better friend for him, in this world, than Maggie, whether she knew it yet or not. "What do you want?" he asked, as they opened the other containers on the table.

"Besides all of the aforementioned?" Maggie helped herself to some kung pao chicken.

Gabe nodded as he savored the taste of fried Peking dumplings.

"Freedom, I guess, to say and do what I want, when I want, how I want."

Gabe made a mental note not to push Maggie into anything she didn't want from here on out. "What else?" he asked seriously, able to tell from the look on her face they were getting to the heart of things.

Maggie looked him straight in the eye, and stated softly and firmly, "I want to know any marriage I am in will last—the way my parents' marriage did. They loved each other and were totally committed to each other until the day they died. I want that, too, Gabe.''

''As do I,'' Gabe replied solemnly. He knew better than anyone that children needed both a mother and a father. He had lived through the heartbreak of a broken marriage and a broken family and knew it was better for children if parents weren't divorced.

Maggie swallowed hard, pushed her food aside. ''We're talking about making some pretty big promises here, Gabe,'' she warned, lifting her gaze to his.

Gabe took in the sudden trembling of her limbs. ''That scares you, doesn't it?'' he observed gently.

Maggie lifted her slender shoulders in an elegant shrug. ''Doesn't it scare you?''

''Not as much as being without you does,'' he said. He stood, drew her into his arms, and smoothed the tousled hair from her face. ''You don't have to give me an answer tonight, Maggie.'' He kissed her lightly, persuasively. ''Just think about it. Think about the life we could have if only we gave this marriage a real chance.''

Chapter Twelve

Maggie awakened in Gabe's bed, knowing she had been very very thoroughly loved the night before and feeling every inch his wife. She lay quietly for several minutes, savoring the warmth and strength of his body wrapped around hers.

"You're thinking about it, aren't you?" Gabe said, his hands softly stroking her hair.

Her heart brimming with tenderness, Maggie snuggled closer. She loved the warmth and solidity of his chest, and the tender way he held her in his arms. She kissed his shoulder. "You've made it impossible for me not to think about it."

Gabe shifted his weight and rolled onto his side. He bent his elbow and propped his head on his hand as his eyes met and held hers. "Does that mean you're leaning toward saying yes?" he asked softly.

Of course she was thinking about saying yes, Maggie thought wistfully. She wanted to be Gabe's wife—in the real sense—more than anything in this world. She just wasn't sure they had the kind of passion that could last. That kind of passion required love. And thus far, though she knew she was indeed in love with Gabe, he had not once mentioned the feelings in his heart.

Not sure, however, that an enduring love for her wouldn't well up in his heart, given more time, Maggie remained silent. She had pressured her first husband into marrying her, into eloping, and had ended up with only disaster on their wedding night, when it turned out he didn't love her after all. She didn't want to ruin her blossoming relationship with Gabe. She wanted to let their feelings grow naturally and just see what developed.

Uncertain, however, how to explain all that to Gabe, without making him feel guilty and prompting an ultimately false but well-meant declaration of feeling from him, Maggie bit her lower lip, took a deep breath.

The phone rang.

"Saved by the bell." Maggie blew out a sigh of relief and grinned as she reached for the phone, and handed it to him,

Reluctantly, Gabe put the receiver to his ear, murmured a sexy hello. He listened, then said, "Hi, Mom. No, you didn't wake us. What's up?" He paused again. "Sounds fine. Yeah, Saturday night it is." He hung up. Clamped an arm about her waist and drew her closer once again. "Since we didn't want a reception or a wedding, the family has decided they are throwing a beach party in our honor tomorrow evening,'' he told her as he fitted one of his hair-roughened legs between hers. ''It's going to be at Chase's.''

Maggie groaned as she thought about the last round of Deveraux betrothal parties she had attended—on Chase's arm. ''Any chance we could forget to attend?'' she asked, not sure she wanted to remind anyone of that.

An exasperated expression on his face, Gabe traced her lower lip with the pad of his thumb. ''I have a feeling Luis, Enrico and Manuel would come looking for us if we did.'' His expression sobered and he dropped his hand, and sat up, looking ready—albeit reluctantly—to take on the day. ''Mom invited them and their families, too. And—'' he slanted her a warning glance over his shoulder ''—she asked me to tell you to fax her a complete list of everyone you want invited to this shindig no later than noon today, so they can give everyone enough time to make plans to attend. She also wants to know if we want to register for gifts.''

Maggie tugged the sheet around her breasts, shook her head. ''No. That would feel dishonest.''

Without warning, Gabe shifted again, so he was lying over top of her, his legs braced on either side of her. He propped his weight on his elbows and framed her face with his hands. ''It wouldn't have to be, if you agreed to make our marriage a real one," he prodded softly.

Maggie caught her breath as her heart swelled with unspoken love. She steadied herself and searched his eyes. "I don't want to rush things," she said quietly.

"We're not." Looking all the more masculine and determined, Gabe bent his head and kissed her then— her eyes, her lips, her hair—until she believed in the promise of their future as much as he. Tenderness welled in his eyes, his low voice. "The truth is, Maggie, I should have pursued you and made you mine a long, long, long time ago."

"YOU LOOK HAPPY," Manuel told Maggie when he and his brothers arrived to begin work on Gabe's kitchen once again.

I am happy, Maggie thought. *Happier than I had ever dreamed of being. And it's all because of Gabe. And the wonderful, womanly way he's made me feel.* "As well I should be," she said, deliberately misunderstanding the unspoken implication behind Manuel's remark as she spread grout over the ceramic tiles she had set the evening before. "This job is going great. And we're almost right on schedule."

Manuel turned his head sideways, and studied her from that angle. "Somehow, I think it's more than that," Manuel drawled in a low, teasing voice.

"Mmm-hmm," Enrico agreed, visibly pleased.

"She really is glowing," Luis said affectionately.

From all that lovemaking last night and again this morning after we awakened, Maggie thought.

"Are you sure you're not pregnant?" Manuel said, stepping nearer and studying Maggie even more closely.

Maggie froze self-consciously, despite her efforts to project an outward cool. "What would make you think that?" Maggie said, trying not to flush.

"Just the way you look," Luis decided, after a moment.

Enrico nodded. "That's the way my Maria looks, every time she is with child. Sort of blissful and full of hope and happiness."

Which was, Maggie thought, exactly the way she felt, despite the fact Gabe hadn't once said he loved her, or even come close.

Aware the guys were waiting for an answer, and that they had become the only family she had in the year since her parents' death, Maggie admitted reluctantly what she would not have even discussed otherwise. "As far as I know, I am not pregnant," she confessed with a disappointed frown.

"But you wish you could be," Manuel said.

Maggie ducked her head and continued spreading the grout with slow, deliberate strokes. "I know you guys love me, but I really don't want to talk about this with you, okay?" she said.

She didn't want even to think about the possibility of her and Gabe having a baby until it was real. She felt as if she was wishing and hoping for enough as it was, in just wanting him to love her as much as she loved him

To her relief, the guys sighed, shrugged and eventually got down to work, too.

Maggie finished the tiles, then went back to her office, wrote up and faxed off the guest list to Grace. Only then—unable to help herself—did she walk into the bathroom and open her medicine cabinet. There, on the top shelf, was the home pregnancy kit she had bought herself the day she had decided to try and become pregnant, husband or no husband.

What if Luis, Manuel and Enrico were right? she wondered nervously.

What if she was already pregnant with Gabe's baby?

Wasn't it time to find out? she wondered as she picked up the box and turned it over to look at the instructions.

Or should she wait another day or two or three?

MAGGIE COULDN'T SAY why it was, except that she was afraid her mysterious new glow was all due to her love for Gabe—but she didn't want anything spoiling her newfound happiness, including the knowledge she wasn't yet pregnant. So she put the box back in the medicine cabinet, and decided the test could wait another week or more.

What she wanted now was simply the joy of being with Gabe.

Besides, she reasoned, the tension and anxiety of becoming a real Deveraux—in the minds of his very protective and loving family—was challenge enough for one weekend.

"You're nervous, aren't you?" Gabe said, as he and Maggie got ready for the crab feast at Chase and Bridgett's beach house.

"Why would you say that?" Maggie asked, as she slipped on a pair of tangerine slacks and a striped tangerine-and-white boatnecked top with three-quarter-length sleeves.

Gabe grinned in amusement as he spread shaving cream on his face and jaw. "Because," he explained as he reached for his razor, "that's the fourth outfit you've had on in the last half hour, we're ten minutes late already and you're still nowhere near being ready to go."

Maggie went into the adjacent bathroom to watch him shave. Her back to the mirror, she perched on the opposite edge of the double sink. "What if it turns out bygones can't be bygones?"

Gabe shrugged his broad shoulders carelessly. "They already are, remember? You went to a Deveraux party a few weeks ago. That welcome-home gig for Bridgett. Everyone was very cordial to you."

Yes, Maggie thought, they had been. But then she

hadn't expected them to be rude—the Deveraux clan was far too classy and polite for that. Unfortunately, in Maggie's estimation, the situation wasn't as simple as Gabe would like to think. She watched Gabe shave with long, careful strokes of the blade. "I was on your brother's arm that night."

Gabe rinsed the razor, and started on the other side of his face. "He just took you to the party and then handed you over to me. And that was to show everyone that he no longer held any grudges."

Maggie inhaled the minty smell of his shave cream. "I know."

"Everyone was nice to you that evening, weren't they?" Gabe continued conversationally, as he shot her a baffled glance.

"Very nice," Maggie conceded.

"Then…?" Gabe tilted his head up and drew the blade beneath the underside of his jaw.

Figuring her hair had been in hot rollers long enough, Maggie took her hair down and dropped the curlers, one by one, into the case on the counter. "I hadn't run off and secretly married you then, and caused a little mini-scandal that your parents had to deal with."

"So?" Gabe shrugged as Maggie ran a brush through her hair, arranging her curls in a bouncy, face-framing style. "They would have only been mad at us if we had ended up in the tabloids, made things even more difficult for my mom in the wake of her being fired from the network and dragged the Deveraux name through the mud. Thanks to our boffo appearance on the 'Rupert and Casey Show' that didn't happen.''

Determined to be practical about this, even if Gabe wasn't, Maggie put her brush down on the counter. ''But a scandal could still erupt if anybody found out how and why we really got married,'' she said firmly.

Gabe splashed water on his face, then blotted it with a towel. ''No one is going to question why we eloped,'' he said, just as resolutely, as he poured aftershave lotion on his palms and rubbed it over his face.

Inhaling the brisk sandalwood-and-spice fragrance clinging to his face, Maggie hopped down from the counter. Unable to help noticing how handsome Gabe looked in just khakis, she tore her eyes from his bare muscled chest and met his eyes once again. ''How can you be so sure?'' she said softly, wondering why she was the only one of them who had a persistent sense of impending disaster nagging at her.

Gabe placed his hands on her shoulders. Abruptly, he looked as deeply satisfied as he did whenever he was gallantly rushing to someone's rescue, or solving a medical problem for a patient. ''Because all people have to do is look at us to know that our marriage has become a real and joyous one, in every way,'' he told her in a low, self-assured voice. ''And there's no tabloid story in a happy marriage—no reason for familial disapproval. Therefore, because we have finally fixed things between us, there's no reason for any-one—including my parents or the rest of my family—to be unhappy with us.''

As much as Maggie was loathe to admit it, Gabe had a point. All Tom and Grace Deveraux had ever wanted for any of their kids was for them to be happy and productive. Once that criteria was met, they had no complaints. Ditto the rest of the Deveraux clan. She shook her head at him, even as she basked in his supremely confident grin. ''You're awfully sure of yourself,'' she teased.

''Sure of us,'' Gabe corrected, as he caught her around the middle, brought her against him and de-livered a scorching kiss that soon had her insides tin-gling. ''Now come on.'' He took her by the hand, and led her into the bedroom, where he quickly tugged on his shirt. ''Let's get this show on the road! And get the party started!''

To GABE AND MAGGIE'S mutual relief, the Deveraux family welcomed Maggie every bit as warmly and enthusiastically as Gabe had predicted they would. Maggie's fears abated, she immediately relaxed and began to enjoy herself.

Satisfied the evening ahead was going to be a pleasant and cordial one, Gabe left Maggie talking kitchens with his mother and went off with Chase to help build the fire where they would cook the evening meal.

"How is Jane Doe doing?" Gabe's aunt Winnifred wandered over to ask as soon as they had selected the spot for the fire.

"If all continues to go well, she's going to be released day after tomorrow," Gabe said. Seeing Luis, Enrico and Manuel and their families arrive, Gabe lifted his hand in a wave. They all waved back and then began unloading food from their vehicles. Smiling, Maggie directed them up the steps and into Chase's beach-house kitchen, where Bridgett and her mother Theresa Owens were supervising the set-up of the casual buffet.

"Any idea yet who she is?" Jack Granger asked as he moseyed up to join the group on the beach.

Gabe shook his head as he lowered his shovel and began digging a pit in the sand. He paused to fill both his aunt and his friend in on the appearance of the red-haired girl who had left the note stating that Jane Doe did have a family—the family just didn't know they were related to Jane Doe.

"I don't suppose you've figured out who the red-haired girl is," Tom Deveraux said, as he too joined the conversation.

Gabe shook his head as he and Chase continued to dig a hole big enough for the fire. "We've had all the fourth-floor nurses on the lookout for her, but she hasn't shown up to see Jane Doe. Not that they are aware of, anyway.'' There were no guards on the fourth floor, so anyone could slip in and out.

"What about the request for information at the TV station? Has anyone come forward with pertinent information?'' Gabe's mother asked.

"No," Gabe released a frustrated breath. "So they finally stopped running it."

"What about Harlan Decker?" Jack Granger asked. "Has he come up with anything yet?"

Gabe shot a glance at Maggie—who seemed to be having a great time up on the deck—talking to Chase's new wife, Bridgett, and her mother.

Gabe paused, thinking how lovely Maggie looked, with her cheeks all flushed and her blond curls ruffled by the wind, then he reluctantly turned his thoughts back to those gathered around him, and the conversation at hand. "The last time Aunt Winnifred talked to him, he thought he might be getting close," Gabe said.

"Well, I for one would really like to see Jane Doe united with family," Grace said, as she carried a load of kindling over and set it down on the sand.

Gabe lifted his brow in amazement as he and Chase began building the fire. He turned to his mother. "You've met her, too?"

Grace nodded. "I stopped by the hospital the other day. I wanted to meet the genteel lady who had gotten so much press, yet still remained a mystery."

Winnifred turned to Grace and asked curiously,

"Did Jane Doe put the sheet over her head when you were talking to her?"

Grace shook her head, adding, "But then she didn't look at all familiar to me, the way she did you."

"Maybe Jane was afraid you'd identify her if you spent too much time talking to her or looking at her," Amy suggested, as she brought over the cast-iron cooking grate that would rest atop the fire.

"She does seem to want to keep her identity a secret," Gabe admitted, as he fitted the kindling in between the larger chunks of wood. Although he really couldn't figure out why, unless Jane Doe feared she might be declared mentally incompetent to manage her own affairs and/or put in a nursing home against her will by well-meaning or greedy relatives.

"Do you think this Jane Doe knows who she is?" Harry, Aunt Winnifred's butler, asked, as he brought over a bucket of crabs ready for cooking.

"I'm not sure," Gabe allowed. He stepped back while Chase lit the fire. "But one thing is certain—Jane Doe is holding back a lot more than she is telling, in hopes of staying in the hospital a few more days."

"Can't you keep her hospitalized?" Amy asked sympathetically as the fire slowly took hold. "Just until she trusts us enough to confide the details of her situation, whatever it is."

Gabe shook his head in mute disappointment. "The rules about that are pretty strict," he told his family honestly. "We can't keep anyone who isn't sick in the hospital. And the hospital needs the bed."

"Then she's completely recovered?" Grace asked, in obvious relief.

Gabe nodded. "Her pneumonia has cleared up. Unfortunately, she still needs to be off that sprained ankle for another seven to ten days. So wherever she goes, she'll have to have someone take care of her."

"And if Jane Doe can't arrange that?" Amy asked.

"Then she'll probably be sent to the county nursing home," Gabe said. Which was exactly where Jane had not wanted to end up.

"Well, I'll talk to her again tomorrow morning," Amy said determinedly, "Maybe we can figure something out."

"Thanks," Gabe said, knowing his little sister was nearly as much of a Good Samaritan as he was. "I'd appreciate it."

Deciding he had been separated from his bride far too long, Gabe made his way toward the deck of Chase's beach house. Before he was halfway there, Luis, Enrico and Manuel intercepted him. "We've got coolers of soft drinks in the back of my SUV," the burly Manuel said, slapping Gabe on the back. "Why don't you come and help us carry them in?"

Gabe looked at the three Chavez brothers. Obviously, they had something they wanted to say to him. Out of respect for Maggie and because of the Chavez brothers' love of his wife, Gabe would hear them out. But he would do so in private.

"We just wanted to say we're all glad you listened to us and did Maggie right after all," Luis began enthusiastically as soon as they had rounded the side of the house, en route to where all vehicles were parked.

"We know you weren't too keen on the idea of marrying her. At least in the beginning," Enrico added quickly.

"But you did, after we talked to you, and for that we are all grateful," Manuel concluded sternly. "Maggie most of all."

Luis nodded and continued with a disapproving frown. "You hurt her before."

"You cost her a husband and a baby, when you broke up her plans to marry your brother Chase," Enrico agreed.

"But now you've made things right in marrying her and doing whatever it took to make her happy again. And for that," Manuel said gravely, as he extended his hand, "we all want to congratulate you."

"Just so you know, I'll continue to do whatever it takes to make Maggie happy," Gabe promised soberly. "I figure I owe her that much at least," he admitted, doing his best to reassure Maggie's protectors, as the soft thud of footsteps sounded on the concrete behind him.

Realizing they were no longer alone, Gabe turned, saw Maggie standing there, a stricken look on her face. He didn't need a crystal ball to realize she had heard practically everything that had been said, and misunderstood every single word of it.

"Actually, Gabe," she said with a haughty look that cut straight through his heart, "you don't owe me anything at all."

Chapter Thirteen

Luis, Enrico and Manuel looked just as stunned as Gabe felt as Maggie turned on her heel and stalked away from them.

Able to see they were about to go after her, knowing they would only make things worse with any well-meaning words they might say, Gabe held up a hand to stave them off. "I'll handle this," he said.

He lengthened his strides, and caught up with Maggie as she headed around the side of the beach house next door, and down the beach.

"You misunderstood," he said, as he matched his steps to hers.

"Really," she mocked him dryly, as she slanted him a glance and kept going, cutting through the waving strands of sea oats and marching across the dunes that separated the homes from the Atlantic Ocean. "I thought I understood you perfectly." She shook her head in bitter self-admonition as tears gathered in her eyes. "My only regret is it took me so long to realize why you were so willing and eager to help me have a baby in the first place.''

Knowing they'd never get anywhere unless they talked about this openly and honestly, Gabe clamped an arm about her shoulder and stopped her headlong flight. "I would have done it whether Luis, Manuel and Enrico pressured me or not," he said.

"And why is that, Gabe?" Jerking free of his touch, Maggie spun around to face him. "Because you still felt so guilty about breaking up my marriage to Chase?" she demanded, incensed. "Or because you knew my chance for having a baby at all might well have passed me by?"

The situation was bad, Gabe told himself, but not unsalvageable. And it wouldn't be unless he lost his head. Patiently, Gabe explained, "You were never meant to marry Chase, because you didn't love him. And as for the other, you're not infertile yet."

She speared him with a censuring, holier-than-thou gaze. "You're sure about that?" she countered sarcastically.

His manner as calm and deliberate as hers was overwrought and emotional, Gabe said, "Call it instinct, but yes, I think you'll have a baby. Probably sooner than you think."

Maggie looked more hurt than ever, but no more ready to reconcile with him. "That would be a big relief to you, wouldn't it?" she guessed sadly.

"Try joy," he suggested, advancing on her, not

stopping until they were nose to nose, "and yes it would be a very happy occasion for me. For us." He cupped her shoulders gently with his hands, looked down into her face. "I want to have a child with you, Maggie. I want to have a real marriage with you." He paused, swallowed around his guilt. "A baby won't erase everything bad that's happened in the past." Like the pain he had caused Maggie, when he had initially pursued and then deserted her. "But it will bring us both a great deal of joy in the future. It'll help us make a fresh start, just like this marriage will."

"Well, thanks," Maggie said, standing as still and unresponsive as a statue in his arms, "but I don't want to be the recipient of a mercy marriage any more than I want to continue to indulge in lovemaking as an act of kindness."

More frustrated than he could ever recall being in his life, Gabe let her go, stepped back. He shoved his hands through his hair. "There was nothing kind about what I did for you in the bedroom, Maggie. Don't you get that? It was selfish from the get-go."

Bright spots of color appeared in her cheeks. "Because you lusted after me."

"Yes." Gabe saw no reason to sugar-coat that. "From the very first moment I saw you, I knew I wanted you to be mine and no one else's. I just didn't let myself think I could have you for a while. But once the family strife involving your broken engagement to Chase was cleared up, once you had recovered and were no longer on the rebound, I knew the field was wide open again.''

''And yet,'' Maggie stared at him angrily, ''even after Chase gave us his blessing, you didn't come after me.''

Gabe shrugged, not sure he could explain that to anyone's satisfaction. He had just known it wasn't the right time. Not then. ''Things were awkward initially. You were on edge every time you were around me. To be honest, I wasn't sure we would be able to get past that, but we did.'' To the point he had been fairly certain she was falling as deeply for him as he was for her. But now, seeing the bitterness in her eyes, hearing the rejection in her low tone, he wondered if that were true.

Maggie threw up her hands, paced a short distance away, before turning back to face him. ''The point is, Gabe, if I hadn't called you that day a few weeks ago and asked you for advice on my medical problems, you never would have stopped by my beach house, and talked to me, and you certainly never would have kissed me again.''

Gabe remembered that day. She had been so distressed. Crying. He'd had no choice but to take her in his arms, and try and calm her down, and once he had, well—the urge to kiss her had been as strong as the need to take air into his lungs. Unfortunately, at the very moment he had kissed her, they'd heard a car driving by, and had looked up and seen Chase. And the anger on Chase's face, and the guilt he and Maggie had both felt at that point, had driven him and Maggie apart once again and kept them apart for several more weeks. But now Chase was happily married to Bridgett, the Deveraux family had put aside their discord over the way Maggie Callaway had once come between Gabe and Chase, and, as far as Gabe and everyone else who knew them was concerned, there was no reason for him and Maggie ever to be apart again.

Figuring Maggie was not very likely to see it that way at the moment, however, Gabe decided to save them both some grief and take a less direct approach. "Next thing I know you'll be saying I asked Penny Stringfield to find a way to get herself blackmailed and start a fire in my kitchen just so I'd have an excuse to spend more time with you." *Why did it matter anyway, how and why and when they had gotten together, as long as they were together, anyway?*

Maggie released a pent-up breath. "You're missing the point," she told him in a low, upset voice.

Gabe searched her face, and found only anguish in her pretty green eyes. "And that point would be?" he ground out the words between his teeth.

Maggie shrugged her slender shoulders as if it didn't really matter to her either way. "That our getting together was as much accident as anything else."

"It was fate," Gabe disagreed strongly. Irritated

she could be so quick to pretend their relationship was just another not-so-important event in their lives, he crossed his arms in front of him and regarded her in mounting frustration. "And that's the way these things happen," he explained grumpily. "It's the way everyone gets together, in crazy, convoluted ways that don't bear analyzing."

She shot him a deeply skeptical glance and took another step away from him. "You're sure I wasn't just another in a very long line of good deeds?"

Frustrated to find his common-sense words had had zero effect on her, Gabe jammed his hands on his hips and demanded impatiently, "What are you talking about?"

"I know how you operate, Gabe, and so do you. You see someone in trouble, you help them, regardless of the cost to yourself, and then you move on to the next person you need to assist."

It was Gabe's turn to shrug. "I've never denied that." Helping people gave him immense satisfaction in both his professional and personal lives. It was also a way to make up for any past sins.

Maggie's eyes filled with overwhelming sadness, and her face twisted with pain. "Only in our case, you upped it another notch, thanks to the well-meaning but misguided pressuring of Enrico, Manuel and Luis, and you not only helped me find a doctor to diagnose my problem, you married me and tried to give me the baby I wanted so badly."

"We both want a baby," Gabe said sternly, flabbergasted that she could think he was so shallow and short-sighted. "And this is different from every other Good Samaritan action I have ever undertaken." It was different than any romance he had ever had!

"No, Gabe, it's not," Maggie said, the tears she'd been holding back spilling over and running down her face, "and that's why I'm ending this farce of a marriage after all." She put up her hands to keep him from taking her in his arms again, and deliberately backed away, her look warning him not to even try and touch her. "Because sooner or later you are going to realize you've completed your good deed with me, the pleasure we felt today will fade, and you'll want to do what you always want to do when you've completed your act of chivalry, and move on." Her voice broke, and pain spilled through them both, as Maggie concluded hoarsely, "And I don't want to be around when you do."

GABE RETURNED to the party alone, and made a beeline straight for his parents. "I've got to go to the hospital," he said.

"What?" Grace did a double take and nearly dropped the serving platter she was setting out on the picnic table on the deck.

"The party is in your honor, son," Tom reminded him.

"I know, but there's a patient I've got to see," Gabe fibbed.

Grace's eyes narrowed in maternal concern. "Where's Maggie?" she asked.

Gabe lifted a hand, turned and walked off, declining to answer a question he had no answer for. "I'll talk to you all later," he said. He didn't have to turn around. He could imagine the not-so-surprised-after-all looks on his parents' faces. They had probably expected a romantic reversal like this all along. The only real surprise was that he hadn't.

He'd never had any luck interesting Maggie in being with him over the long haul. He didn't know why he'd ever thought now would be any different, even if she was still wearing his wedding ring on her finger. She probably just wasn't the marrying kind. Hence, her breakup with Chase before their wedding, her breakup with him after theirs. All along she had been looking for an excuse to maintain her independence while still getting the baby she wanted. And, that being the case, Gabe decided grimly, he should go where he had a real chance of making a positive difference in someone's life. Not somewhere he was simply a means to an end. So he headed to the place he always went when he needed to do some good—the hospital.

"Hey, Gabe!" Penny Stringfield greeted him cheerfully twenty minutes later, as he stepped onto the fourth floor. Looking happier and more relaxed than she had in weeks, the petite nurse hurried over to him. "I can't thank you enough for what you did this morning," she said.

Gabe paused, almost afraid to hope he had been successful in his late-morning visit to her estranged husband, given the way things had been going for him. "Lane called you?"

Penny nodded, and confirmed, "Right after you went to see him at the TV station. He asked me to lunch and we talked, and the bottom line is, we're going to see a marriage counselor and try again."

Gabe's shoulders relaxed. "I'm glad," he told Penny sincerely. Gabe had hoped Lane would listen to what he had to say on the importance of allowing each other to make mistakes—apparently, Lane had.

"We wouldn't be reconciling if you hadn't stepped in the way you did," Penny said softly, her gratitude shining on her face.

"I was happy to help," Gabe retorted quietly. Although, Gabe thought, with no small trace of irony, now that he had helped Lane and Penny put their marriage back together, it was his own that was falling apart.

Penny studied him. "What's wrong, Gabe?"

"What do you mean?"

"I've known you for a long time. Usually, when one of your good deeds reaps positive benefits," Penny continued thoughtfully, "you look like you're on top of the world, or something. But this time, you don't look all that elated.''

Maybe because, Gabe thought, he had finally realized that he needed to do more than solve other peoples' problems. He needed to start working on his own. But that was hard to do, when Maggie wouldn't listen to what he had to say, or cut him the least bit of slack. Like his parents before him, Gabe thought bitterly, Maggie was all too willing to just call the relationship quits, rather than struggle to work things out.

''But then,'' Penny continued slowly, still sizing him up cautiously, ''maybe you don't want to talk about it.''

''Actually,'' Gabe said, ''I don't.'' *Not with anyone but Maggie.* Sighing, he thanked Penny for her concern, assured her that he was definitely going to be fine—as soon as he did something worthwhile for someone else, that was—and continued on down the hall.

''I didn't expect to see you at the hospital on a Saturday night,'' Jane Doe said, when Gabe walked into her hospital room. ''Especially since you were supposed to be at a family party tonight, weren't you?''

Gabe wished he could run into just one female tonight who wasn't interested in sizing up his emotional well-being. ''How did you know that?'' he casually asked his patient.

"Your sister Amy was in here earlier. She said your whole family was going to celebrate your new marriage."

"Well, I'm not here to talk about that," Gabe said gruffly, as he paused to look over Jane Doe's chart. "I'm here to talk about what is going to happen when you're released from the hospital tomorrow afternoon."

Gabe didn't want to transfer Jane Doe to the county nursing home, but unless the genteel lady started co-operating with them, or agreed to his suggested solution, he might have no choice.

Jane flashed him an elegant little smile. "I already know what I want to do," she said, folding her hands in front of her.

This was a good sign, Gabe thought, impressed. Prior to this, all Jane Doe had wanted to do was stay in the hospital—indefinitely.

"I want to go home with you," Jane said.

Gabe did his best to contain his shock. "I'm not your family, Jane," he reminded her gently. "I'm your doctor."

"I know. But you're also a very nice man. And I have no place to go."

It would be so easy, Gabe thought, to do this for Jane Doe. Take her in. Let her stay at his place, at least for a few days, while they hired private detective Harlan Decker to help them discover who Jane Doe really was, and if indeed she did have a family of her very own. Playing the part of the Good Samaritan—in combination with his work at the hospital—would take up all his energies, monopolize his spare time. It would help him forget about Maggie and the mess he had obviously made of their relationship once again.

But if he did that, Gabe knew he would be running away from the best thing that had ever happened in his life.

So, as much as he wanted to help Jane Doe, he knew he was going to have to decline.

"Actually," he said kindly, "we've had two other offers of help for you. One is from my sister Amy. But I think you would actually be better off with my aunt Winnifred. She has a much larger place, and a butler—Harry—who lives in, in addition to other staff who come in to clean and cook daily."

Gabe expected an argument from Jane Doe—after all, she had put the covers over her head the first time Winnifred had tried to visit her, and feigned sleep every other time Winnifred tried to help.

Instead, Jane Doe smiled—almost approvingly. "I suppose it really wouldn't be fair to ask a newlywed to have a houseguest underfoot, now would it?" Jane said.

Not, Gabe thought realistically, given the chore he had ahead of him.

MAGGIE COULDN'T say why—she only knew she was compelled to find out the truth.

The moment she got back to her beach house, she went upstairs to the bathroom in the master bedroom, and took the home pregnancy kit out of the cabinet.

Minutes later, she knew the results of the test.

She didn't have the answer about what to do next.

Fortunately, she had the whole evening ahead. Not sure what she should be feeling at that moment—happy, upset, relieved, discouraged, overjoyed—she sat on the edge of the tub for a while, trying to absorb the momentous turns her life had taken over the course of the last few weeks, then went back downstairs to make herself a cup of tea. And that was when she saw Gabe coming up the steps of her deck with Luis, Enrico and Manuel, their entire families, and the whole Deveraux clan right behind him.

Maggie took one look at their very determined expressions and knew Gabe had done the impossible—he had gotten every single one of them on his side.

She crossed her arms in front of her and braced herself for whatever it was that was coming next.

"We want you to come back to the party," Grace Deveraux began.

Tom Deveraux nodded. "The food will be ready soon. And we want both of you there to enjoy it with us."

Enrico, Manuel and Luis and their wives backed up Gabe's parents. "We mean it, Maggie. We all decided we would give you about fifteen minutes to clear this up on your own. Then we're coming back—

and giving the two of you a joint counseling session if necessary.''

Maggie's jaw dropped. She turned to Gabe in astonishment. ''You agreed to this?''

''I not only agreed—I instigated it.'' He turned to all those gathered behind him. ''Okay, I think I can handle it from here.''

''Fifteen minutes, tops,'' Chase warned them both with a grin.

Mitch nodded as he linked hands with his wife Lauren. ''Then we're all coming back.''

Amy's eyes twinkled optimistically as she smiled. ''One way or another, you two, we are celebrating your marriage tonight!''

The families trooped off.

Deciding it would be undignified to argue with Gabe in front of everybody, Maggie leaned against the waist-high wooden enclosure on her deck, and folded her arms in front of her contentiously. ''I can't believe you did that,'' she said.

''I can't believe I waited an hour before I did that,'' Gabe said right back, as their families disappeared from view. He gave her a smile so wicked it made her heart race as he closed the distance between them, and continued in a low, supremely confident voice, ''Marriage, as you know, is not something to be taken lightly. And even if you didn't mean your vows at the time you made them,'' he reminded softly, as he took her all the way into his arms, "you did mean them later."

"How do you know that?" Maggie asked, as she tilted her face up to his.

Gabe's blue-gray eyes softened seriously as he smoothed the hair from her face, and traced her lower lip with the pad of his thumb. "Because I saw the way you looked at me, and I felt the way you kissed me and made love to me." He paused to search her eyes. "Tenderness like that doesn't come out of nothing, Maggie. Tenderness like that comes from the deepest recesses of the heart."

"I admit I have feelings for you," she said hoarsely, knowing it was now or never. If she was ever going to have a future with Gabe, she was going to have to let her guard down. Forget about the possibility of being hurt or abandoned and trust Gabe to be everything she had ever thought him to be, whether he said the right words at the right time or not. Because, bottom line, words didn't make a man. Actions and character did. And of those, Gabe had plenty of both.

"I have feelings, too," Gabe interrupted, before she could continue telling him all that was in her heart.

"I know you desire me," Maggie said thickly. *Just as potently as I desire you.*

Gabe frowned. "I'm talking about more than that, Maggie. I'm talking about love. Admiration—"

Maggie stopped moving, thinking, breathing, and just blinked in raw amazement. "What did you say?" she demanded incredulously.

He wrapped his arms around her and brought her closer yet, until they were touching in one electrified line. "That I love you, Maggie. More than I ever imagined I could love anyone."

"Oh, Gabe." Maggie wreathed her arms about his neck and went up on tiptoe. She touched her lips to his. "I love you, too."

They kissed again and again, until both of them were nearly overcome with emotion.

"Tell me there'll be no more walking away from each other," Gabe prodded, still holding her in a way that left no doubt about the depth of his commitment to her. "Tell me—from this moment on—that you're willing to give this marriage your all. In good times and bad. No matter how confusing or tense things get. Tell me you'll stay with me and help us to work things out."

Her heart overflowing with love, Maggie kissed Gabe back, until she was sure he understood how much she adored him, too. "I promise, as of right now, I am every bit as committed to this marriage, and to our love, as you are," she said softly. Then stopped for another blissful kiss. "But Gabe—?"

"Hmm?" All the tenderness she had ever dreamed of radiated in his low, sexy voice.

"One more thing." Maggie swallowed hard as she

splayed her hands across his chest. "About the baby we were trying to have—" she started in a voice that shook.

Mistaking what she was about to say, Gabe silenced her with a finger to her lips. He looked down at her, eyes serious. "Listen to me, Maggie. I want to have a family with you more than anything in the world. But if it doesn't work out, if we find out we can't get pregnant after all, we'll adopt. And we'll have our family that way. The important thing is for us to love each other and be together," he said firmly. "In the end, that's all that matters."

"Oh, Gabe," Maggie said as the wistfulness of her dreams translated into the reality of the present, "I want that, too."

They kissed again, chastely this time.

Gabe's eyes were dark, intense as he tightened his grip possessively on her waist. "And I promise— from now on, I'm putting you—us—first," he told her solemnly. "No more filling up the hours with endless good deeds. I still plan to be one of the good guys, but as for my heart, and my soul, they belong only to you."

"And mine belongs only to you," Maggie said, just as confidently, as she felt all her dreams come true, at long last. "But about that family—" she began tremulously once again.

Gabe stopped, looked into her eyes.

"I just took the test." Maggie swallowed around

the growing lump of emotion in her throat. "Your gut feeling was right," she said, her eyes misting with tears of happiness. "We are going to have children together. I'm pregnant."

"Oh, Maggie," Gabe whispered, all the joy she felt reflected on his face. They hugged each other fiercely, then indulged in a long, steamy kiss that left them feeling glowing and alive, and very much man and wife. Eventually they headed back down the beach to Chase's house and the party in their honor.

Gabe sighed contentedly as he wrapped an arm around her. "It looks as if three of us Deveraux offspring now have found the loves of their lives. Only one of us is left to be matched up."

"Amy," Maggie said, as she thought of Gabe's spirited baby sister. Like Maggie, Amy was a very successful businesswoman, but not so fortunate in her romantic life.

Gabe tightened his grip on her waist and slanted her a glance. "Think she'll be matched up soon?" he asked Maggie thoughtfully.

Maggie smiled, wrapped her arm about his waist, and snuggled even closer to his side. "I really hope so."

"In the meantime, we've got a party to attend."

As they neared Chase's beach house, Maggie and Gabe saw Harlan Decker drive up. Maggie and Gabe met him at the edge of the drive.

"Sorry to interrupt the party," the casually dressed

private detective said, as he paused to put out his cigar, "but I'm looking for your aunt Winnifred."

Figuring this had to be about Jane Doe's identity, Gabe caught his aunt's attention and waved Winnifred over. Winnifred radiated excitement as she swept across the lawn to join them. "I take it this means you found out what I wanted to know," Winnifred surmised happily.

Harlan Decker nodded matter-of-factly, opened the manila file in his hands, and withdrew a photo of a young woman with long red hair. "Is this the girl you saw on the deck?" Harlan asked.

Gabe and Maggie nodded. "That's her, all right," Gabe said with satisfaction. "Did you find out who she was?"

Harlan shot them a sober glance. "Her name is Nicole Hyatt. She's the granddaughter of the housekeeper who took care of your Jane Doe in a secluded location until the grandmother died, then Nicole took over on a part-time basis. But Nicole's been struggling with it because Nicole's in college and hasn't been able to be there to take care of your Jane Doe, the way her grandmother once did."

"Why didn't she simply notify Jane Doe's family?" Maggie asked.

Harlan shrugged. "Jane Doe forbade it, and Nicole Hyatt felt she had to honor that. If someone else discovered it, however…well, Nicole felt that would be okay. You have to understand. Nicole was pretty desperate. And she wants Jane Doe to be well taken care of by someone who can give the old lady the time and attention she warrants.''

Gabe paused, absorbing that. Although the reasoning was a bit convoluted, it all sounded honorable thus far. ''Did Nicole tell you who Jane Doe was?'' he asked curiously.

''I'd already figured that out on my own, by the time I talked to Nicole,'' Harlan said.

''How?'' Winnifred interjected, amazed.

Harlan opened the manila file again and took a handful of pages. ''I took the newspaper photo of your Jane Doe and used my computer to reverse the lady's age. Here she is at ages sixty, fifty, forty, thirty and twenty.'' As Harlan talked, he handed over the photos one by one. ''Look familiar?'' he said, as they reached the last photo of a beautiful dark-haired woman.

Winnifred looked down and caught her breath. ''Oh, my heaven!'' she gasped, laying her hand across her heart.

''I take it this means you recognize her?'' Gabe asked his aunt.

Winnifred nodded, then announced in a low voice that shook, ''Our Jane Doe is none other than Eleanor Devereaux! Eleanor isn't dead, after all!''

How to Marry A HARDISON

by Kara Lennox

continues this December in

AMERICAN *Romance*®

SASSY CINDERELLA

After an accident knocked him off his feet,
single dad Jonathan Hardison was forced to hire
a nurse to care for him and his children.
The rugged rancher had expected a sturdy,
mature woman—not Sherry McCormick,
the sassy spitfire who made Jonathan wish
their relationship was less than *professional*....

**First you tempt him.
Then you tame him...
all the way to the altar.**

Don't miss the other titles in this series:

VIXEN IN DISGUISE
August 2002

PLAIN JANE'S PLAN
October 2002

HARLEQUIN®
Makes any time special ®

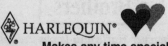

Coming in December from

HARLEQUIN®

AMERICAN *Romance*®

and

Judy Christenberry

RANDALL WEDDING
HAR #950

Cantankerous loner Russ Randall simply didn't need
the aggravation of playing hero to a stranded
Isabella Paloni and her adorable toddler. Yet the
code of honor held by all Randall men wouldn't
allow him to do anything less than protect
this mother and child—even marry Isabella
to secure her future.

**Don't miss this heartwarming addition
to the series**

Brides
for Brothers

Available wherever Harlequin books are sold.

HARLEQUIN®
Makes any time special ®

HARRW